lullaby *

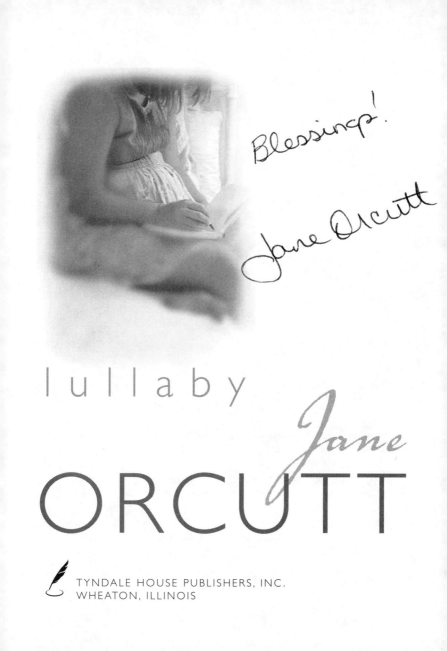

Blessings!

Jane Orcutt

lullaby

Jane

ORCUTT

TYNDALE HOUSE PUBLISHERS, INC.
WHEATON, ILLINOIS

Edited by Diane Eble

Designed by Julie Chen

Published in association with the literary agency of Janet Kobobel Grant, Books & Such, 3093 Maiden Lane, Altadena, CA 91001.

This novel is a work of fiction. Names, characters, places, and incidents are either the product of the author's imagination or are used fictitiously. Any resemblance to actual events, locales, organizations, or persons living or dead is entirely coincidental and beyond the intent of either the author or publisher.

Library of Congress Cataloging-in-Publication Data

Orcutt, Jane.
  Lullaby / Jane Orcutt.
    p. cm.
  ISBN 0-8423-5405-0
  1. Teenage pregnancy—Fiction.   2. Childlessness—Fiction.   3. Adoptees—Fiction.
I Title.
  PS3565.R37 L85 2002
  813'.54—dc21   2001006433

Printed in the United States of America

07 06 05 04 03 02
9   8   7   6   5   4   3   2   1

to Sandra Byrd

Merrilee Hunter dug into the pockets of her ragged maternity cutoffs and laid the haul on the drugstore's glass counter: a provisional driver's license, one quarter, one dime, two nickels, a piece of string from the hem of the shorts, a half-empty tube of Avon lipstick, and a scrap of paper with a phone number. The paper she hurriedly stuffed back into her pocket, as though the saleswoman on the other side knew exactly what it was.

In a bony ninety-degree angle, the woman leaned over the counter, sifting the money from among Merrilee's possessions, pushing each coin with the pad of her index finger into a pile. "Twenty-five, thirty-five, forty-five." She raised her eyes, then folded her arms against the glass. "You ain't got enough, Merrilee," she said, her voice quivering with triumph. "Popcorn'll cost you forty-nine cents."

Merrilee bit her lip. She slid her open palm across the counter to gather her things, but old man Kenner stepped up beside her and stopped the motion with his gnarled, white-haired hand. Four pennies plunked against the glass. "I'll spot her the rest, Paula Jean. Just go get a bag from the machine before her bus gets here."

Paula Jean bustled toward the other end of the counter, fixing Merrilee with a wrinkled frown as she shoveled the popcorn into a red-and-white-striped bag.

Merrilee eased her hand out from under the old man's, ducking her head. "You didn't have to do that, Mr. Kenner," she mumbled. "I can do without."

"Let's just call it one of them bone voyagee gifts, okay, girl?" His gaze dropped to her extended belly, which pressed up hard against the glass counter. He caught her glance and smiled, a leer she recognized well. "Ain't ever' day a girl like you runs from town, tail tucked. Now your mama, I coulda seen her doing something like this, but not you. Thought you had more spunk."

Merrilee's face warmed, but she didn't respond.

One, two, three . . . take deep breaths, Merrilee. Don't let anybody see how you feel.

The baby poked against the counter as if to break free. Merrilee stepped back.

Mr. Kenner squinted. "You headin' out to look for that baby's daddy? None of the boys round Palmwood here have fessed up, and they generally brag on accomplishments like you're displayin' so proudlike."

Merrilee didn't answer. He didn't really want to know the truth; that was devoured by gossip in this small town as easily as the Laundromat dryers ate up the precious quarters Mama used to hoard in her tip jar.

"Here's ya popcorn." Paula Jean shoved the bag across the counter, her hands stopping well shy of Merrilee's.

"Thanks." Merrilee lifted the bag, then looked Paula Jean and Mr. Kenner square in the eye, hoping for some sort of friendly sign, some expression of farewell. They stared back at her, eyes cold and hard as the iron gates of Palmwood's cemetery slamming shut.

"Well . . ." She gestured toward the door. "Guess I'll wait outside for the bus."

"You do that, hon." Paula Jean wiped down the counter. "Say, Ed, what do you think about the Gophers' chances this fall with their new quarterback? That kid can throw a mighty long pass, I hear."

"Well, now . . ." Mr. Kenner leaned on the counter and launched into a verbal assault on the upcoming team.

Merrilee hefted Mama's battered blue hard-sided suitcase and headed outside. A bell chimed as she exited.

Never send to know for whom the bell tolls; it tolls for thee.

She smiled wryly as she eased down on the

wooden bench below the ancient metal Grey-
hound sign.

Mama would've said the bell was some sort of
omen—but good or bad? Her superstitions
didn't always make sense, and as far as Merrilee
could tell, had no basis in any folklore other
than that of her own creation.

"I'm tellin' you, Merrilee," she'd said, pointing with her freshly lit Marlboro for emphasis.
"Our lives are ruled by chance. Luck. The best
we can do is watch for signs."

"Oh, Mama."

"It's true, girl. Heed the bad ones and grab
on to the good ones."

Merrilee decided to humor her. "But how
will I know the difference?"

"You'll know." Mama had taken a long drag
of the cigarette, blown out the smoke, then
ruffled Merrilee's hair. "You'll just know."

It seemed to Merrilee that up until the past
seven months, all her knowing had been pretty
easy. She'd found, if not all her answers, then
most of her peace, at the ramshackle Gospel
Fellowship Church building just up the road

from the trailer park. When Merrilee was big enough to buckle her own patent leather Sunday shoes, Mama walked with her every week to the church. She'd smile down at Merrilee over an ancient hymnal the Baptists and Methodists had handed down. Merrilee would tuck her hand in Mama's and prop her own hymnal against the back of a splintered pew, gaping at the giant wooden cross down front. Pastor Luke gestured at it every week, at the end of the last hymn before he launched into his sermon. "Can you hear him, brothers and sisters?" he might say, after the final verse of "Softly and Tenderly." "Oh, sinner, he's calling you home!"

After a few years, Merrilee grew to understand why the wooden boards were prominently displayed up front and why some church members danced and clapped their hands with joy during the hymn singing. Mama always just rolled her eyes and smiled smugly, still believing in luck and good versus bad signs. One Sunday morning after a long night out with one of her boyfriends, Mama cracked her bedroom door, a washrag at her forehead, just long enough to pronounce herself a retired churchgoer.

From then on, eleven-year-old Merrilee walked the dusty path alone every week to the Gospel Fellowship. One Sunday, when Pastor Luke gave the altar call and the choir sang "I Have Decided to Follow Jesus," she also walked alone down front and accepted the significance of the wooden cross into her life.

The members of Gospel Fellowship accepted her as well. They never asked about Mama but welcomed Merrilee as family. Her new brothers and sisters walked and talked with her along the spiritual road, pressing a Bible into her hands, prayers into her ears, and hope into her heart.

Another kick from the baby, and Merrilee's smile faded to a frown. She set the striped bag aside, fluttered a hand over her belly, then reached for the suitcase. Instead, she settled back, folding her hands in her lap.

Later, on the bus. When it's quieter, and I can think a bit.

"Merrilee!"

Sylvie Ponds, Palmwood's only librarian, huffed and waddled her way across the gravel parking lot. Face flushed with exertion, she fanned her hand against thin bangs slicked with sweat against her forehead. The sleeves of her polyester polka-dot blouse strained at her doughy biceps.

Merrilee smiled. "Mornin', Miss Ponds. I told you there wasn't any need to see me off."

Sylvie heaved herself down on the bench, sucking in gulps of air like a landed catfish. Merrilee grabbed the popcorn and scooted all the way to the end of the bench, till one hip hung off. She braced her feet hard against the ground and held on to the edge of the seat, between her knees. The baby kicked, but she ignored it.

"I was . . . afraid I'd miss you, Merrilee." Sylvie drew one last gulp, then laid a hand over her ample chest as her normal breath returned. "I couldn't have you leave without my saying good-bye, now could I?"

"I'm glad you came." Merrilee glanced at the drugstore's entrance, then back again. "Truth to tell, I'm kinda scared, Miss Ponds. Mama always said someday we'd get to travel, but I never figured I'd be doing it like this. I feel like I'm sneaking out of town."

Or being run out on a rail.

Sylvie patted her hand. "This is a good Christian place where you're going. They'll take fine care of you. I'll miss you over at the library every week, but the books'll be waiting for you when you get back." She cleared her throat. "And if not those at the Palmwood Library, why, those at another one. Just you keep reading, hear?"

"I will, Miss Ponds," Merrilee said solemnly, though she could no more stop reading than she could stop the birth of this baby. Reading library books took her beyond the dingy trailer she had shared with Mama, but reading the Bible took her even further—beyond herself. Of all the Gospel Fellowship members, Sylvie Ponds had encouraged Merrilee the most in this direction. In quiet moments at the children's table at the library, they had huddled in undersized plastic chairs to study passages of Scripture. Especially the ones about God's love and mercy, which Merrilee clung to, even now.

Sylvie squeezed her hand. "What you're doing—"

She blinked hard, then tried again. "What you're doing is about the most selfless thing I ever knew anybody to do."

Embarrassed, Merrilee looked away.

A large silver bus pulled into the parking lot, splaying gravel, its destination shining plainly above the driver's head: Austin. Merrilee thought it might as well have said Exit.

She rose, gripping the worn handle of the suitcase in one hand and the popcorn bag in another. "I guess this is it," she said, trying to smile.

Sylvie rose too, shading her eyes against the sun. "You have a safe trip, okay?" She paused, lowering her voice. "You're a good girl, Merrilee. Don't let anybody tell you different."

Merrilee nodded, but her heart sank clear to the bulge in her belly. She tried to speak, but the words caught in her throat. Where would she have been the past few years without Sylvie Ponds? She couldn't have made this difficult decision without her guidance and love, especially now that Mama was gone and nearly everyone else had turned away.

The doors to the bus hissed open, and the weary-looking driver trudged down the stairs. He held out his hand for Merrilee's suitcase in a gesture of bored impatience.

Sylvie patted Merrilee's shoulder, then pulled her into a quick hug. They'd never touched before, and Merrilee felt the awkwardness between them as wide as the baby that separated them from a full embrace. Sylvie stepped back quickly as if she felt it too, then smiled lopsidedly. "Go on with you, then. Go see what they got to offer in Austin. Try to make it to the capitol if you can."

Merrilee nodded.

"And drop me a postcard!"

The driver stepped forward. "Miss? Your bag?"

Merrilee clutched the handle tighter. "I'll just carry it with me, thanks."

He shrugged and headed for the bus. "All right, but we need to get going."

Merrilee followed, then turned. "Bye, Miss Ponds. Thank you for . . ."

Sylvie smiled. "It's okay, Merrilee." Her voice

softened. "It'll be okay. I'll be praying for you. 'Where two or more are gathered . . . ,' remember?"

Merrilee glanced over her shoulder and saw Paula Jean and Mr. Kenner standing in the drugstore doorway. Neither waved; neither smiled. There goes Faye Hunter's daughter, their faces said.

Merrilee turned away and boarded the bus. She bumped and jostled her way down the narrow aisle, past four other souls who stared listlessly out windows with no latches. She took the seat farthest back, next to the bathroom, then cradled the suitcase and popcorn bag against herself. She closed her eyes and didn't open them even when the bus shifted from gravel to pavement and lumbered down the two-lane road.

When she knew they must be well out of town, she propped the popcorn bag against the armrest of the adjoining empty seat, then balanced the suitcase on her knees. She popped open the rusty clasps, then pulled out a ragged pastel cloth journal and a pen. Making a desk of the closed suitcase, she opened the book to the next white page, blank and crisp.

Nipping the cap off with her teeth, she poised the pen over the paper for a moment, then wrote slowly and carefully, the way Miss Percy had taught her all the way back in second grade.

Dear Baby Girl,

In all my fifteen years of growing up, I never once thought about what it'd be like for a new mama to leave the hospital with her baby in another pair of arms. I guess I've always fancied the notion of a perfect family, with the daddy beaming over his wife and new child, maybe even a grandma or two hovering nearby, knitting booties or something.

I don't know why I think like that, since I never even knew my own daddy. All Mama ever said was that he'd loved her, but not enough to stick around. Except for times like father-daughter banquets, I never really missed having a daddy, though. I had Mama. Or at least I always thought I'd have her.

I've prayed a lot about what I'm doing,

and this seems to be God's answer. Pastor Luke thought so, when I talked to him about it. So did Sylvie Ponds. They're the only two folks in town who don't look sideways at me for carrying you. Even Mama had her druthers about your life . . .

Merrilee paused long enough to scoop a left-handed fistful of popcorn into her mouth. She started to write more, but the achy place inside her heart simmered like water on a back burner. She carefully placed the pen in the journal's gutter and set the suitcase and book in the next seat, then wiped her greasy hand on her shorts.

Tucking her legs up under herself awkwardly, she curled up into the seat and stared out the window. Her face reflected back in the finger-print-smudged glass, and she glanced away. Anyway, the prairie grass and scrub cedars looked the same as they did around Palmwood and probably wouldn't give way to anything prettier before the bus got to Austin.

Mama had been to Austin several times, she'd

told Merrilee. Once when she was in a high school track meet—she'd been pretty good back in her day at jumping the hurdles and running sprints, she'd bragged. Another time with some man for a weekend, just for a lark.

Mighta been my daddy, for all I know. Maybe that's where they brought me into being. Wouldn't that be funny, me bringing this baby back to be born where I came from?

Merrilee popped open the suitcase again and slipped her hand inside the frayed elastic side pouch, fingers digging for the carefully trimmed photo she'd downloaded at the library. The paper was already worn around the edges from too much handling, even though she'd never shown it to anyone, not even Miss Ponds.

She squinted at the photo, trying to pretend she'd never seen it before. As if she'd just turned the page of a picture album and come across this couple with their dog—which is exactly how she'd found them on the Internet through the Palmwood Public Library's lone computer. It'd taken her days to work up the courage to even access the Austin adoption agency's Web page, but once she had, she'd listlessly paged through image after identical image of smiling, hopeful couples.

Merrilee fingered the scrap of paper in her pocket. They had no idea she was even on her way. The agency said she could call them when she got to town if she wanted to wait. It was her decision, they said. All the arrangements were hers to decide.

Merrilee shivered. She squeezed her eyes shut and wrapped her arms around her thick waist, swaying slightly to a gentle hum.

" 'Jesus loves me, this I know. For the Bible tells me so. . . .' "

✳ ✳ ✳

Nora Rey clasped her hands in her lap and stared straight ahead. She felt Steven cover her hands with his own, as he did every year at this time.

In the past she'd thought it'd be easier to stay home and pretend to relax with the Sunday newspaper, but that had never proven beneficial. It didn't hurt any less than publicly facing what many might whisper was a private inadequacy.

Father Thomas smiled down the aisles at the members and visitors of St. Mark's Episcopal Church. "This day is always special in the lives of our church families. We honor what is perhaps the most honorable and truly—in my book—oldest profession."

The congregation laughed. Many women nodded their heads in agreement. Steven's hand tightened over Nora's, as though he could feel the building ache in her heart.

Father Thomas smiled broadly. "I call it a profession because according to many women, it's a job. But ladies, it's a calling."

The emptiness in Nora's heart expanded.

"Would the mothers of our church please rise?"

Church bulletins, hymnals, and Bibles were audibly set aside as all around Nora a sea of women rose—great-grandmothers leaning proudly on canes, grandmothers with oversized handbags, middle-aged women whose teenage children looked away in embarrassment, young women with infants in their arms or toddlers tugging at their skirts.

Pregnant women who laughed as their rounded bellies bumped the backs of pews.

Nora stayed seated and blinked. A second time, longer.

Lord, oh Lord. Why not me?

"Ladies, you are the hands that rock or have rocked the cradle of our future. On this day, we honor each one of you for your courage, your stamina, and most of all, your love. Please accept these roses as a token of our appreciation and admiration."

Ushers handed a single pink rose to each standing woman. Neil Harrigan, Steven's doubles partner at the club, extended a rose to Nora, his eyes sympathetic. She declined with a quick, polite head shake.

Steven squeezed her hand. The ushers moved on and the crowd of standing women dwindled. When the deacon began the dismissal, Nora slipped out the side aisle, followed closely by Steven.

Father Thomas met them on the steps outside the heavy oak main doors. "It's a hard day for you, I know," he said, touching Nora's shoulder. "I admire you for showing up each year."

"I think I've actually grown accustomed." Nora's laugh sounded hollow to her own ears, and she fished the sunglasses from her Luis Vuitton purse to cover her embarrassment.

"Great message, Father." Steven held out his hand, forcing the priest to release Nora's shoulder.

I owe you, Steven.

Nora pushed the sunglasses to the bridge of her nose and smiled what she hoped was a polite farewell. Steven took her elbow, and they turned.

"Any word from the adoption agency?" Father Thomas halted their quick escape.

"Not yet, but we're hopeful," Steven said. "Sorry to run, Father, but we have to be somewhere."

The doors opened and the congregation spilled out onto the steps. Father Thomas turned away, and Steven deftly steered Nora to their car.

Safely inside the Lexus, neither spoke as they

headed toward the hills west of Austin and the security of home. Nora studied Steven's hand as it controlled the gearshift with masculine firmness.

It was his hands that had attracted her to him, hands so smooth yet confident as they dissected specimens in their biology lab at the University of Texas long ago. Hands that would later perform delicate orthopedic surgery. Hands that would join with hers on their wedding day, and for twenty-three years since, but that could never do enough to fill the emptiness of her arms.

After fulfilling their career plans, Nora and Steven had celebrated their fourteenth anniversary by ceremoniously tossing the little round packet of pills away. Then thirty-six, Nora felt ripe and attractive, and she and Steven were both certain a child would soon result from their purposeful intimacy. God had always blessed them.

But the years passed, one after another, in a succession of torn calendar pages and monthly tears of failure. Specialists were consulted and options weighed, but even medicine couldn't undo what had apparently been ordained.

"Maybe I've been too selfish," Nora had said. "This is God's vengeance for my wanting to establish our careers first."

Steven had taken her in his arms and stroked her hair, the way he always did to comfort. "God isn't punishing you. You helped me through medical school and residency and built your own real estate career helping people find homes. Why would he want to punish you for that?"

She hadn't been able to answer, but the medical tests all pointed to her own, not Steven's, physical inadequacy. Nora struggled to reconcile her infertility with her faith in a good God who gave children as a blessing. Was her medical condition a curse, or did the Lord intend a higher purpose?

"We may never know the reason," Steven said. "But we have to walk by faith."

Nora smiled wryly. "I feel more like I'm crawling."

"At least we're moving forward."

Renewed, Nora had agreed to fertility treatments. Perhaps this was all a spiritual test, rather than a curse. But after two unsuccessful years, Steven tentatively broached the subject of adoption. Nora gratefully agreed, relieved to abandon the heart-wrenching pain of each month's failure. Surely *now* God would grant her a child.

Yet three years of waiting had passed—marked by daily, rather than monthly failure—as younger couples were repeatedly selected by birth mothers to be the parents of their children. Apparently Nora's adoptive clock was winding down as rapidly as her biological one had.

Steven pulled off Ranch Road 2222 and onto the gravel road that wound its way to their lakefront property. He mashed the remote-control button, and the privacy gate swung open. They drove up the road toward the dream home that felt to Nora more like a yellow brick shell every day.

Inside the garage, Steven parked the car beside Nora's SUV. She entered the house first, listlessly tossing her purse onto the kitchen counter. Beyond, Lake Travis sparkled through the expansive living room's floor-to-ceiling windows.

She felt Steven's hands on her shoulders. "Want to go for a swim? or a boat ride?"

Nora shook her head. Patient Steven always understood.

"Please, Nora?"

She turned. His forty-sixth birthday was in three months, and while he was still handsome and youthful from tennis, waterskiing, and swimming, he had developed age lines around his eyes. Nora laid her hand against his cheek and smiled. How could she refuse him anything? "A swim in the pool might be nice."

Steven smiled, and the lines deepened. "Put your suit on, Blondie," he said, squeezing her shoulder playfully. "I'll meet you outside." Whistling, he loosened his tie and headed toward the back door that led down the steps to the pool.

Nora grinned, knowing that he'd probably worn his swim trunks under his suit in anticipation of an afternoon outdoors. She wondered what his patients—especially the more conservative, elderly ones—would think if they knew how unconventional Dr. Rey really was.

In the spacious, orderly walk-in closet, Nora changed out of her suit and carefully hung it next to the others. She pulled on her favorite swimsuit, the size six white maillot that best complemented her tan, then scooped up a beach towel. Pulling back her hair with a terry-cloth band, she followed Steven's trail of shoes, socks, suit coat, pants, and tie as she passed through the kitchen and hallway. Fingering the collar from the shirt hanging on the back-door knob, she smiled.

Outside, Lucky bounded toward her and barked an enthusiastic greeting. The German shepherd wound around Nora, bumping against her hips. He nuzzled his head against her hand. Laughing, she rubbed his ears affectionately. "Poor old Lucky. You think you're a cat, don't you?"

At the sound of her voice, he sat back on his haunches and stared at her imploringly.

"Lucky!" Steven called. Quickly transferring his affection, the dog loped down the grassy slope toward the swimming pool. Steven threw a tattered tennis shoe across the slope, and Lucky gave chase.

"Thanks." Nora descended the stairs to the pool area. "Sometimes his affection can be—"

"Annoying?"

"Embarrassing."

Steven grinned and dived into the pool. He bobbed to the surface and flipped onto his back, whistling "How Much Is That Doggie in the Window?"

Nora draped her towel over the back of a chaise lounge, then slathered her arms with sunblock. She leaned over to apply lotion to her legs, and when she straightened, Steven was treading water in the deep end, watching her.

Nora turned to the CD player and popped in Billie Holiday. She rested her fingers on the machine as it crooned "Lover Man." When she turned back to the pool, Steven was still watching her.

Nora moved to the edge of the water's deep end and studied the bouncing reflection of the sun and the ripples of light at the bottom of the pool. Up from the lake behind her roared the sound of a boat, punctuated by squeals of children being towed on an inner tube.

Closing her eyes, Nora hooked her toes around the rough concrete edge, bent her knees, and leaned forward. She broke the surface cleanly in one fluid movement.

Underwater, life hung suspended, muted. She pushed back to the surface in long, clean strokes, and when she broke free, Steven was waiting beside her.

"You looked like Katharine Hepburn in *The Philadelphia Story*," he said. "Nice dive."

Nora started swimming away. "Thanks, Cary Grant. Race you to the shallow end."

"Hey! No head starts!" Steven splashed after her, and they reached the pool steps at the same time. Breathless, they fell across each other in a wet tangle, laughing.

Nora leaned back against Steven, resting her head against his shoulder. He loosened the hair band with his fingers, fanning her hair against the water. She closed her eyes, feeling her stomach tighten as his fingers trailed the strap of her swimsuit.

"Nora," he said softly. "About today . . ."

"Shh." She'd nearly forgotten, in the sweetness of being at home. Of being with the man she loved on a warm day in a pool beside a beautiful lake, listening to Billie Holiday wail her sorrows.

She had so many blessings—was it selfish to want more? And yet motherhood, so basic, so biological, didn't seem to be part of God's plan for her life. His purpose was larger than her desires, yet not having even a glimpse of his blueprints was often so difficult.

Show me. Please show me.

"I love you," Steven whispered into the curve of her neck. "We're in this together."

She squeezed her eyes shut, the ache rising to her throat. "Steven . . ."

The poolside phone rang sharply, slicing the moment. Steven exhaled with resignation and released her. "It's probably about Mrs. Wimbers and her hip replacement. When I saw her on rounds yesterday, she was having a lot of pain."

He grabbed the phone and a towel at the same time, already rubbing his hair. "Steven Rey."

The water lapped against Nora's too-flat stomach, and she extended her arms for balance. She turned her head against the glare of sunlight across the pool's surface, winking back tears.

"No, we didn't know." Steven bent to scribble on a pad of paper. "We'll check it out. Yes. We'll contact you as soon as possible." He set the phone back on the table, then stared out at the lake.

Nora sighed. The day felt broken, ruined. "Trouble?"

Steven turned, a goofy grin on his face, like the day the dentist had given him nitrous oxide to remove an impacted wisdom tooth. "We've been chosen," he said.

She stared blankly. "Chosen for what?"

"Chosen as adoptive parents. A birth mother saw us on Adoption Lifeline's Web site and moved into the agency just yesterday. They called to say she'd left us an E-mail. Nora! She wants to talk to us about raising her baby."

Lucky charged across the grass, barking,

chasing a squirrel up into an oak. He planted himself at the bottom, wagging his tail in invitation for play.

Another boat roared past, followed by a Jet Ski.

Nora drew a deep breath, tightening her arms to maintain her balance. Her heart beat quickly, singing against her ribs.

Another chance. Perhaps their last one, after all the days and months of disappointment.

It'll be a perfect match, this baby and us. It has to be!

Steven walked to the pool steps and held out his hands to help her stand. "Before we call . . . ," he said, squeezing her hands.

"Yes," Nora murmured in agreement, bowing her head as Steven prayed aloud for the young girl and her baby, for their own desire to raise a child. For the first time in a long while, hope filled the voice of his petition.

✳ ✳ ✳

Steven logged on to their Internet service provider, his hands still damp. Standing behind him, Nora curled her fingers around his towel-wrapped shoulders, holding her breath as she leaned over to watch the mail screen pop up.

"We have eleven messages," Steven announced unnecessarily, scrolling through the list.

Nora dragged an antique Windsor chair beside Steven's ergonomic one. "I wonder why she didn't phone."

Steven shrugged, his eyes trained on the screen. "The agency said we can call her. Here's the E-mail, the last one. It's from . . . Fatgirl."

"Fatgirl?" Nora had always pictured their birth mother as a slim, beautiful cheerleader who'd gotten caught up in the throes of passion with an athletic boyfriend.

Steven poised the cursor over the on-screen envelope. "Ready?"

Nora nodded. Steven double-clicked the mouse, and they both leaned forward.

> Dear Nora and Steven,
> I saw your picture on the Adoption
> Lifeline Web page. You look very
> nice. I like your house and your dog

too. Please call me at the agency if
you want to talk. My name is Merrilee
Hunter.

"Merrilee," Nora whispered. It was a pretty, old-
fashioned sort of name. At least it worked to dispel
the image "Fatgirl" evoked. Given the two discor-
dant pieces of information, Nora pictured a stocky
girl with a ponytail, dressed in a gingham shirt and
jeans.

"She didn't give us much to go on." Steven
pushed back his chair, clearing his throat. "Do
you want to call, or should I?"

"We can each get on an extension." Nora
rose, shivering as air blasted from the vent and
chilled her wet swimsuit. "Don't you think we
should change clothes first?"

"She might decide we're not interested and
leave for a while," Steven said, the practical
surgeon taking over.

Nora nodded. "I'll go to the kitchen phone.
Will you do the talking, to start us off?" Negoti-
ating real estate transactions had wrung any
shyness from her personality, but now her hands
shook as she lifted the phone from the marble

countertop. Steven was more accustomed to taking charge in delicate situations.

"They're calling her to the phone!"

Nora pressed the receiver's Talk button just as the phone was picked up at the other end.

"Hello?"

Nora gripped the countertop, her heart pounding. *Say something, Steven. And please let it be good.*

"Merrilee? This is Dr. Rey."

There was a pause at the other end. "Dr. who?"

"Rey. Steven Rey. My wife and I are posted on the Adoption Lifeline Web page. . . . Are you Merrilee?"

"Oh, Steven. Of course! I forgot you were a doctor. You're a doctor of . . . of . . ."

"Orthopedics," he said, then added, "a bone doctor."

"Oh! I see," Merrilee said, though she sounded like she didn't.

Steven cleared his throat. "Merrilee, my wife—Nora—is on the line too."

"Hello, Merrilee," Nora said in the calmest

voice she could muster. What had the adoption agency suggested as an opening line with a birth mother? "How are you feeling?"

"Pretty good. It's kinda hard to sleep at night, what with my belly being so big. But other'n that, I can't complain."

Nora swallowed hard. "How far along are you?"

"Near as I can guess, I'd say seven months."

"You haven't been to a doctor?" Steven said. Nora held her breath, hoping he hadn't offended the girl.

"Not yet. I haven't had the money. But the agency said they . . . well, I guess you . . . would pay for things like that. If we decide to make the swap, that is."

The swap? Nora frowned, walking back to the office where Steven sat. He saw the expression on her face and put a finger to his lips. "The agency said you just came to Austin yesterday, Merrilee," he said. "Where's your hometown?"

"Nearby. Palmwood."

Nora and Steven exchanged glances. Palmwood was scarcely a blip on the highway from Austin to Houston. "Do you like it here

so far? Austin, I mean. And at Adoption Lifeline?" he said.

"I guess so. I'm still settling in. My room's
real pretty."

A muffled popping sound indicated the girl
was probably wrapping the telephone cord
around her fingers. Nora also heard a rhythmic
squeak-creak and realized the girl was sitting in
a rocking chair.

"Merrilee," she said softly, "what made you
contact us today?" She paused. "Did you know
it's Mother's Day?"

The chair's tempo increased. "Yes, ma'am,
I do. I been thinking about my own mama most
of the day. That's why I needed to come to Austin."

"But did you want to come?" Steven said.

There was a pause at the other end of the
line. "Yeah."

Nora drew a deep, happy breath. She and
Steven smiled at each other over their respective
receivers. "Name the day, and we'd be delighted
to meet you," he said.

"I guess Wednesday would do fine. Mrs.
Pennywood wants me to see a doctor."

"Wednesday it is." Steven doodled the word on a pad of paper. "What would you like to do?"

"The agency said sometimes people like to eat supper together or something." She hesitated. "It don't . . . er, doesn't have to be anything fancy. I don't want to impose."

Impose? "We'd be delighted to have dinner with you," Nora said. "We know many wonderful restaurants, and it would be our pleasure to treat you and get to know you. And let you get to know us, too."

"Okay."

Nora gave Steven a thumbs-up sign but was surprised to see him frowning, like he did whenever a patient wasn't being totally honest with him. The girl's tone was definitely more subdued than when the conversation began—did he think she was entertaining second thoughts? Nora started to ask, but Steven again put a finger to his lips.

"Merrilee," he said gently. "There are so many adoptive families listed on the agency's Web page. Why did you choose us to call?"

They heard her draw a soft breath. "Because your dog's name is Lucky."

chapter
TWO

*M*errilee sat cross-legged on her bed and eyed the starchy white curtains of her window. She was still afraid someone would haul her away from the adoption agency's residential home, declaring that she didn't belong.

She didn't. This room with its clean curtains and shining clear window, gleaming hardwood floors, and matching white wicker furniture, was foreign to anything she'd ever had at the trailer. She'd been here three days now and still hadn't unpacked, despite the residential mother's warm assurance that this was, indeed, her home for the next two months.

She rose slowly, fighting the ungainly balance of her body. Smoothing her hair, she peered into the wicker-framed mirror. One of the other girls had loaned her a pair of navy blue maternity slacks and a bright "flower power" shirt to wear for her first meeting with the family that might adopt her baby. The residential mother, Mrs. Pennywood, said it was normal to feel nervous and that she should relax and enjoy getting to know the couple. And most importantly, dear, she should listen to her heart as to whether these were the people she wanted to raise her child.

Merrilee dug into her suitcase, hesitated, then lifted out a Polaroid snapshot of Mama. It was the only photo she had of her mother by herself—one of the few photos she had of her mother, period. The three others either had a then current boyfriend or Merrilee in the picture. Merrilee had trimmed the image of the boyfriends, but Mama always looked lopsided somehow.

In this picture, Mama was holding a beer can in one hand and a cigarette in the other. She was smiling, and Merrilee knew it wasn't one of her fake photo smiles because she herself had taken the picture last summer.

The three of them were barbecuing outside the trailer. Lucas Procter shoved the camera into her hands.

"Get a good picture of your mama now, Merrilee," Lucas said. "Ain't she a dish? This'll give you something to remember her by when you're a mama yourself."

"That won't be for a long, long time, Lucas," Mama said, laughing. She leaned up against the redwood picnic table one of her past boyfriends had stolen from a roadside park. Posing for the camera, Mama smiled at Merrilee. "You're not going to get tangled up with boys for a long time, are you, sugar? Have yourself some fun just being a girl for a while, right?"

Merrilee sighted Mama in the viewfinder and grinned. "Right, Mama." It was their secret conversation, their inside joke kept from Mama's boyfriends. She liked each one of them well enough, but Merrilee had seen over the years, even if Mama hadn't said a word, that men

*weren't always the most reliable creatures God
had ever made.*

*Mama smiled back, holding up the beer can
like a trophy and the cigarette between two
fingers of the other hand. She tilted her head
back and made a pout like a 1930s movie star.
She winked at Merrilee, who was too mesmer-
ized to take the photo. Mama probably wasn't
what most people would call beautiful, but she
managed to snag attention—especially from
men—wherever she went. In her presence,
Merrilee often felt like not only a shadow of
Faye Hunter, but of herself as well.*

*"Snap the picture, Merrilee," Mama said through
her posed expression, and the moment was segmented
from time, frozen.*

Merrilee wedged the photo into the bottom
corner of the mirror's wicker frame, then
touched the image of Mama's face. Beside that
photo she placed the one of Mama and her
together, the one Boone Samson had taken of
them at Merrilee's fourth birthday party at
McDonald's. It'd been just the three of them

at the fast-food place—no streamers, cake, or other kids to celebrate—but it'd been a good party all the same. Merrilee had liked Boone, probably better than any of Mama's other boyfriends, before or since. At age four, she'd foolishly thought that they'd be a real family, but he'd eventually left Mama and Merrilee by themselves, like all the rest.

Merrilee touched the worn leather Bible that had once been Mama's. Merrilee had set it out beneath the mirror when she first arrived here, but she'd been too ashamed to read it alone for a long while now.

A knock sounded at the door, and it swung open. Sheryl Billups stuck her head into the room, followed by the rest of her nineteen-year-old pregnant body. "Hey, girl. Whatcha doing?"

Merrilee stepped away from the mirror. "Just getting settled."

"You've been doing that for three days now," Sheryl said, lowering herself onto the bed and hugging a decorative pillow. "Don't you like it here?"

"It's all right."

"All right?" Sheryl sat up, grinning. "Just wait till you meet the parents. They treat you like a queen around here; these parents are so eager to have a baby, they'll do just about anything you want." She lowered her voice. "Why do you think I'm having a second baby? I learned the first time that a girl can make a little extra money, get a few little trinkets for herself."

Merrilee frowned. "We're not supposed to take gifts. Or money."

Sheryl shrugged. "Who has to know? Besides, the parents are so grateful to you, what does it hurt? It makes them feel good, and you might as well make a little something for yourself for all you're going through."

Merrilee rubbed her belly thoughtfully.

"That's right." Sheryl grinned, watching Merrilee's hand. "You're growing a gold mine there. Take what you can, Merrilee. You've been left high and dry, haven't you? Isn't it nice to live in this place where nobody yells at you and no man comes sniffing around? Yeah, we have to go to a weekly Bible study, since this is a Christian joint, but you seen that swimming pool outside? The meals they serve here? You get anything like that at your home? I sure didn't."

She leaned back. "I may just do this every couple of years. If nothing else it gets me away from Gary for a few months."

"Is that your boyfriend?"

"No, my husband. But he doesn't want kids, so this is the second I'm giving up. I had an abortion four years ago, but trust me, this is the life. Nobody cared about me then. Why, I had to drive myself home from the clinic. My parents called me trash, and my boyfriend never spoke to me again. But let the world know you're planning to put a baby up for adoption and they think you're a saint."

"That's not what it was like for me," Merrilee whispered. "Everybody in Palmwood looked at me hateful-like, the bigger I got. It would have been easier to have an abortion, but Mama—"

Merrilee bit her lip, glancing at the photos on the mirror.

Sheryl eased up from the bed and headed for the door. "Just wait till you meet the couple you chose—that's today, isn't it? They'll treat you so fine, you'll forget all about your hometown, Merrilee. And you just sit back and let them pamper you, okay? You deserve it."

Sheryl shut the door behind her. Merrilee sat on the bed, deflated, her enthusiasm for meeting the Reys dampened. She squeezed her eyes shut, so that she wouldn't be tempted to glance at Mama's pictures again, and prayed hard. When Mrs. Pennywood knocked, Merrilee was still sitting on the bed. "They've arrived, dear," the elderly woman said from the doorway. "They look as nice as their picture."

Merrilee rose, fighting the fear that churned in her belly, all around her baby. "I . . . I'm ready."

"You look very nice." Mrs. Pennywood smiled, smoothing Merrilee's hair.

As she lumbered down the stairs behind the residential mother, Merrilee didn't feel nice. Maybe they'd think she was too fat. Maybe they wouldn't like her clothes. Maybe they wouldn't like the way she talked.

Maybe they'd decide they didn't want her

baby. She didn't think she could go through all those photos of hopeful couples again.

Mrs. Pennywood led her into the closed-off room with the velveteen furniture that Merrilee was afraid to sit on. Mrs. Pennywood used it primarily for important meetings, and its formality reminded Merrilee of a nineteenth-century parlor—something out of *Little House on the Prairie.*

"Here she is," Mrs. Pennywood said, her voice bright as she opened the door.

A man with medium-brown hair and a trim figure, dressed in tan slacks and a colorful sport shirt, straightened from where he leaned against the sofa.

The woman sat on the sofa, leafing through a magazine, her face tense, her mouth set in a tight expression. She looked perfect—blonde hair swept up and back into a stylish ponytail, gold earrings, and a fashionable pink pantsuit. She looked like a cover model, and when she smiled at Merrilee, her lipstick looked perfect, her teeth like a TV ad for toothpaste.

Merrilee smiled, but it felt fake, her teeth

probably showing as large as a horse's. Mrs. Pennywood stepped back, leaving her open and vulnerable. "Hi," she said, and her voice came out as a squeak. She gripped her hands in front of her belly. "I'm Merrilee."

The man moved toward her with a hand extended. "Hi, Merrilee. I'm Dr. Rey . . . Steven." When he shook her hand, his felt firm and warm.

"Merrilee." The woman rose, nodding, then extended her hand. It felt cool and slim, like the rest of her looked. "I'm Nora Rey. We're so glad to meet you."

"Me too," she said, then couldn't think of anything else. She dipped her head, letting her bangs fall into her eyes.

She felt Mrs. Pennywood's hand at her shoulder. "I usually find that the introduction's the most difficult part of the first meeting. You've all passed with flying colors." She laughed lightly, and Steven and Nora joined in. Merrilee smiled and felt her stomach lurch.

"So often a neutral location goes a long way to ease the awkwardness," Mrs. Pennywood said. "Why don't you three go get acquainted? Merrilee, feel free to knock on my door when you get back if you want to talk."

"Yes, ma'am. Thank you." She smiled, feeling a rush of relief. If only talking to the Reys were as easy as talking to Mrs. Pennywood.

"Shall we go?" Steven held the door open, and Merrilee, feeling embarrassed, scurried through. She sensed Nora following behind her at a more mature pace.

Steven headed toward a Lexus, and Merrilee's eyes widened. "Wow! This is your car?"

Steven clicked the security button on his key chain, smiling. "Would you like to ride in the front seat?"

"Sure!" She turned toward Nora, her expression falling. "If it's all right with you, Mrs. Rey."

"Nora," she said, nodding that regal head. "And no, I don't mind."

Inside the car, Steven inserted the key into the ignition. "Where would you like to eat?"

Amazed by the car's interior, Merrilee forgot her nervousness. "Wow! Look at this radio!

This CD player! And tinted windows, even!"
Mama's old pickup hadn't even had air-conditioning, and the AM-only radio had busted
long ago.

From the backseat, Nora leaned between
Steven and Merrilee. "Where would you like to
eat, dear?" she said.

Jolted back to reality, Merrilee panicked.
She tried to think of restaurants she'd seen
from the bus window when she pulled into
town. "Uh, Chili's would be nice." She
fumbled for the seat belt and clumsily buckled
it over her stomach.

Nora's smile looked patient, like one of
Merrilee's teachers when she couldn't come up
with the right answer. "Wouldn't you rather go
to a . . . quieter place? Steven and I frequent a
restaurant that has peacocks on the grounds
and—"

"Peacocks squawk a lot," Merrilee said without thinking, then covered her mouth with her
hand. "I . . . I'm sorry. That was rude. I don't
mind going there."

"Chili's is fine." Steven started the car, and

Nora sat back. Merrilee faced forward, clutching her hands in her lap, unsettled.

All the way to the restaurant, she told herself it wasn't going to work. She was just too different from these people. The agency had stressed that in what they called an open adoption, everyone should get along. After all, they would be sharing the child's lifetime, should Merrilee choose to stay involved. She couldn't, but that didn't change matters.

Settled into a Chili's booth across from the Reys, Merrilee covertly eyed Nora while the woman studied the menu. Merrilee thought she had a pretty face, even prettier than Mama's, then chided herself for being disloyal. She yanked the menu up to cover her own face.

The waiter stood at the edge of the table. "What would you like, Merrilee?" Steven said.

Panic set in again. She hadn't read a word of the menu, but she didn't want to look like someone who couldn't make up her own mind. "Uh, I'd like a Sprite and a hamburger with that hickory sauce. And some onion rings . . ." Maybe she was being too free with the Reys' money. She glanced up at Steven. "If that's okay."

"Sure." Steven turned to the waiter. "Did you get her order?"

"Uh-huh. For you, ma'am?"

Nora firmly shut her menu. "A glass of iced tea and a grilled-chicken Caesar salad. And please go light on the dressing."

"Yes, ma'am. For you, sir?"

"I think a hamburger sounds good, too." Steven winked at Merrilee. "And an order of French fries and a Dr. Pepper."

Merrilee wanted to sink into the booth. Nora had ordered a salad. She probably thought Merrilee wasn't eating healthy enough for the baby.

To her surprise, Nora smiled, leaning forward on her crossed arms. "What would you like us to know about you, Merrilee?"

Surprised by the woman's abruptness, Merrilee sat up straighter. "What do you want to know?"

"Well, I suppose for starters, how old are you?"

"Fifteen." Right now, despite the baby in her belly, she felt like only five.

"Does the father of your baby know you're here?" Steven said. "Has he signed any papers?"

They were really jumping in with the tough questions. "No, sir." Merrilee swallowed hard. "He never knew about this baby. By the time I found out I was pregnant, he'd left town. We finally heard he'd been killed in a bar up in Oklahoma. Got cut up pretty good, from what they said."

"I'm sorry, Merrilee," Steven said. "You must have been devastated."

Merrilee shrugged. "I'm sorry he's dead, but Wayne and I weren't that close."

Nora's eyebrows drew together, and Merrilee hastily changed the subject. "What else do you want to know? I'm about seven months pregnant . . . I think. This baby sure kicks a lot, and I'm carrying it high. Mama used to say those were two signs you were carrying a girl. I hope so because I'd really like it to be a little girl." She paused, fearful that she'd said the wrong thing. "Do you want a boy?"

Nora and Steven looked at each other. "We've never discussed it," Steven said. "We told the agency that we'd accept either gender."

"Oh. Well, I know men generally seem to want a boy."

"It doesn't matter either way," Nora said. "We would welcome and love a boy or a girl. The doctor may want to do an ultrasound . . . sort of an X ray to check on the baby," she added, as if she didn't think Merrilee would understand. "They can often tell whether it's a boy or a girl. Would you like to know in advance, or would you prefer to wait until the baby's born?"

Merrilee hesitated, considering. She hadn't realized she'd be given a choice. "I wouldn't mind knowing," she said. "That way, you could name it in advance. Talk to it and stuff."

"What would you name a girl?" Steven said. "Have you thought about it?"

She shook her head. She and Mama had never gotten around to talking about it.

"What about a boy?"

Merrilee hunched her shoulders. It was nice

of them to pretend they cared about her opinion, but it would be their baby. Not hers.

Nora leaned forward. "Would you want to
name him after his father?"

Did they have to bring up Wayne again? "No,"
she said flatly, then, to stop any further talk,
added, "I don't guess it's my place to be naming
the kid, anyway. You two would do that."

Merrilee paused. "I bet you could pick a good
name for the baby. I like that you named your
dog Lucky."

"You mentioned on the phone that you
picked Nora and me because of that. Why is the
name so appealing to you?"

Merrilee felt a sudden urge to laugh. Maybe
they were afraid she'd want them to name the
baby after the dog. They looked so serious, so
intent on getting to the bottom of something
that seemed so major to them. She supposed
they had a right to worry about who she was,
what her thoughts were, where she came from.
She would have to tell them just enough not to
make them nervous. "Why did you give him that
name?" she countered.

Steven glanced at Nora. "A neighbor of ours, a vet, found him as a puppy by the side of the road between our properties. Probably somebody abandoned him, then tried to run over him. Both his hips were broken. We rushed the dog in and immediately operated. We saved his life, but my neighbor already owned several dogs, so Nora and I agreed to keep him. He's been with us five years now."

"Do you like dogs, Merrilee?" Nora said.

"Not really. Especially if they're big."

Nora glanced at Steven, then at Merrilee. "Lucky's a pretty big dog. He's a German shepherd. But he's as docile as a lamb."

"Oh, I'm not worried about the baby's safety or anything like that. I know you'd take good care of her."

Steven's eyebrows knit together, and Merrilee could imagine him as a doctor puzzling over a medical problem. "But you didn't tell us why our dog's name means so much to you," he said gently.

She struggled for the right words. Most folks didn't understand Mama's thinking or even try to see things from where she sat. "My mother used to say that our lives are ruled by chance and that I should watch for signs to know what to do. The good signs, that is," she added hastily, in case they thought she had a tendency to lean toward evil. "Mama believed those signs were sent by God to guide us. She said that sometimes when she couldn't hear his voice—probably because her ears were too stopped up—he'd talk to her in other ways."

"And you think Lucky's name is some sort of sign?" Nora said.

Merrilee glanced down at the paper place mat, focusing on the cartoonish chili pepper to keep her composure. She didn't want to cry; she wouldn't cry. "It just hit me that if you thought your dog was lucky, how much more would my baby be, if you were to raise her. She needs a good home with good parents."

"What do your parents think about your pregnancy?" Steven said.

"I don't have a daddy, and Mama . . ." Merrilee drew a deep breath and focused on the pepper until it blurred. "Mama died just about a month ago."

She felt a cool hand on her arm, and when she glanced up, she was surprised to see tears in Nora's eyes. "I'm so sorry, Merrilee," she whispered. "You're a brave girl."

Merrilee smiled. "That's what Miss Ponds says. She's Palmwood's librarian and just about my only friend."

Nora glanced at Steven. "Do you spend a lot of time at the library?" he said.

"Oh yes! I work there part-time, but even when I'm not working, I'm usually down there looking at magazines and books. Or the Internet. That's how I found Adoption Lifeline when I decided this baby needed a home."

"When did you decide that, Merrilee?" Nora said softly.

Merrilee glanced down at the place mat again. "Right after Mama's funeral." She drew a deep breath, then looked up. "If you don't mind, I need to ask some questions of my own now. I read this book called *Adoption Guide for the Average Joe and Jill,* and it said the birth mother should ask certain questions too. I've got 'em memorized."

Steven smiled at Nora. They clasped hands

above the table, and Nora suppressed what sounded suspiciously to Merrilee like a giggle, only she wouldn't think a woman like Nora Rey had ever giggled in her life. "What?" Merrilee said, feeling heat rise to her face. "Don't you think I should ask a few things about you two as well? I'm not giving this baby to just anybody."

"Of course not, Merrilee," Steven said, sobering, glancing at Nora.

Nora took Merrilee's hand. "I'm sorry. We didn't mean to offend you. It's just that we read the same book too and made a mental note on the way over here of what we should ask."

Merrilee smiled. "You must like books."

"We like to read," Nora said. "And yes, we have an extensive collection of books at our house. They feel like old friends."

Merrilee felt a rightness settle in her stomach. "So you'd read to the baby? That's really important to me. I want her to love reading as much as I do."

"We'd read every night before prayers and bed," Nora said. "And during the day too. I'd start with simple picture books, and as she grew older, we'd move up to Dr. Seuss and Little Golden Books, then chapter books. I'd do everything I could to ensure that she loved reading, but I would never force her to read. It should be a pleasure, not a punishment."

Merrilee let out a deep breath. "I'm glad to hear you say that. I hated when teachers would do that to kids who didn't like to read. Seems like it just made them hate reading more."

The server brought their food, halting the conversation. Merrilee dug in, carefully chewing and swallowing the hickory-sauced hamburger with pleasure. She hadn't eaten one since the last time she'd visited Mama at work at the café. Over the years, Mr. Gleason, the owner, had always welcomed Merrilee, even occasionally given her lunch on the house. But that last time, Mr. Gleason had stayed back in his office, as far from both of them as possible. By then, most of the town behaved likewise, what with Merrilee starting to stick out so obvious-like. She wasn't the first unwed teenage girl in town, but she was the only one who didn't have a boy step forward and claim responsibility. The town treated her as if the whole thing were her idea alone.

Or at least hers and Mama's.

Merrilee wiped a glob of sauce from the corner of her mouth and studied the Reys. Nora sat as straight as Merrilee's principal, Mrs. Beecham, always did, leafing through her salad as though she were looking for something in particular. Steven dug into his hamburger with gusto, caught Merrilee's eye, and winked. "You can ask those questions anytime," he said.

She smiled. He wasn't much like any of Mama's boyfriends, though some were nice enough. He didn't look at her like he wanted her to get lost or at least fetch something for him—a pack of cigarettes or a cold beer from the fridge. Yet Steven Rey wanted more from her than anyone had ever asked—this baby, the only thing on earth she had to give, the last thing she wanted to part with.

"Uh, well, now I've forgotten what the book said," she said, angry that she'd lost the questions she'd worked hard to remember.

Nora laid down her fork. Her school principal expression cracked, and her whole face seemed to open up like a moss rose to sunlight. "Speak from your heart," Nora said softly. "Let's forget about the book—all of us."

"Well, okay." Merrilee knew the questions she really wanted answered, but the book—and the Reys—would probably label them as too childish for a pregnant girl to ask: Will you love my baby? Will you teach her to swim so that she won't be afraid of the water? Will you take her to see *Sesame Street on Ice* and the circus and the rodeo, but will you also hold her hand and keep her from going places where she shouldn't, no matter how old she is?

"How long have you been married?" she heard herself say and knew that the book's advice hadn't strayed too far from her.

"Twenty-three years," Nora said. "We met at the University of Texas and married right after we graduated from college. Steven went on to medical school, and I eventually got my real estate license."

"So schooling would be important to you?" Merrilee stuffed a bite of hamburger into her mouth, wishing that her heart could truly speak for her head. She already knew the answer; she already knew *all* the surface answers these people would give. They were meant to be parents. They would be good parents.

"Education is very important to us," Nora said.

"So you won't be working anymore?"

"No. I'll give up my job just as soon as we have a baby."

Merrilee knew Nora hadn't particularly meant her as part of that "we" but that she meant any baby they might adopt. But she knew in her heart they were talking about her child, that the moment she was born, the Reys' life would forever change. And so would her own.

She set down her half-eaten hamburger, suddenly no longer hungry. Her hand rested on her stomach, and the baby kicked. Nora's eyes caught the movement, and she glanced at Steven, who had seen it too. A brief expression of love passed between them, and they clasped hands. They beamed at Merrilee, who suddenly felt like the stray cat she'd adopted long ago.

"I fixed up a box for her like you said, Mama. When will she have the kittens?"

Mama studied the box where Merrilee had set it, smack-dab in the middle of the trailer's living room. The cat kept trying to escape the box, and Merrilee just as persistently pressed her back in. "Move the box to the back of my closet, Merrilee, where it's nice and dark. Then leave her alone, hear? Don't be hovering over her. She wants a little peace and quiet while she does her thing without us bothering her."

"But I want to watch the kittens being born!"

Mama shook her head, putting a sympathetic arm around her daughter. "She'll know just what to do, darlin'. God gave her the instinct to be a mama, and that's just what we're going to leave her to do."

"Education's real important," Merrilee said to the couple who wanted her baby. Her mouth felt dry and raw as a broken chicken bone, and she sipped from her Sprite. She knew Nora was still studying her, and she wanted to slink under the table so that her belly wouldn't be stared at anymore.

"What about you, Merrilee?" Nora said. "Do

you plan to go back to school after your baby's born?"

You're darn right it's my *baby,* she wanted to say, then caught the sympathy in Nora's eyes. This woman was getting under her skin. Just when Merrilee wanted to dislike her for coveting her baby, Nora had gone and asked a nice question.

"I guess I'll finish school," she said.

"And after that?" Nora persisted, but still in that nice, calm tone.

Merrilee shrugged. She hadn't had much time to think about what she'd do after the baby was born and gone, but she did know instinctively she'd have to keep busy. "If Miss Ponds will hire me permanent at the library, I guess I'll become a full-time clerk."

"Did you ever think about going to college? To study to become a librarian, instead of just a clerk?"

Merrilee licked her lips. "Yeah, I've thought about it. But I don't guess I'll have the money."

"There're always scholarships and grants," Steven put in. "At least think about it. Look into it."

Merrilee shrugged. College was out of her future. Working at the library would be a good enough life. Certainly better than Mama'd had it, working at the café, living off the tips she hoarded in a jar. Surely after a while, people would forget about the past. At least once she graduated from school in a couple of years. Until then, the boys would no doubt be after her all the time.

"Where will you go after the baby's born?" Nora said. "Aren't you too young to live by yourself?"

Oh, if Nora Rey only knew. She'd been too young for so long, but she'd been forced to be the adult for more years than she could remember. She'd done more than her share of cooking and cleaning, even taking over the management of the tiny bank account when she was twelve.

"I don't know," she said, hoping they'd leave off asking about her and stick to the subject of the baby. She crossed her arms defensively.

Nora noticed the action and leaned back, setting space between them. "I'm sorry if I pried, Merrilee. It's none of my business."

Merrilee didn't reply, but she relaxed her arms. Nora just seemed concerned. Merrilee would have to watch that, or she'd let down her guard too quickly, too easily. Best the Reys not know the whole truth about things. "Miss Ponds said I could move in with her," she said, tossing the couple a bone to throw them off the scent. "Look, I know what the book said. You've got every right to worry that I'm going to change my mind and keep this baby. I've got several strikes against me—I was raised by a single mother, I'm only fifteen, and I don't have any immediate plans. But I ain't going to change my mind, so just rest easy. Focus on the baby."

Your baby. Not mine.

They nodded, and Merrilee settled back against the vinyl booth. She focused on the dancing chili pepper again until the wetness in her eyes dried away.

＊ ＊ ＊

Dear Baby Girl,
I met your parents today. Their names are
Steven and Nora Rey, but you know that, by

the time you're reading this. They're wonderful people, and I know you're going to be happy with them, as happy as I was growing up with Mama.

The Bible says lots of good things. Honor your father and mother, for one. I always tried to do that with my mama, and I know you will too. Steven and Nora will be different, though. They'll have money for you. Which can't buy happiness, everybody knows, but Mama used to say it could sure put a down payment on it. The rest was up to the man who held the mortgage.

Be happy no matter what you do, Baby Girl. My mama taught me that. There were lots of folks who resented her happiness because of who and what she was, as if her life was the reason for her joy. I knew it wasn't. I saw her cry time and again when some fella would stick around for a while and things would be good for both her and me; then he'd leave, and her heart would be broken yet again. Until that last time, she'd cry for a night, though, then be her old self the next day. "Joy comes in the morning, Merrilee. Don't the Bible say so?"

Steven and Nora will bring you joy all the time, Baby Girl, and not just because of their money. Steven's a real nice guy—I can tell. He'll treat you right and look out for you. He'll make sure the boys act decent and don't take advantage. And Nora—well, she seems a bit icy, but she's got a good heart deep down, I know. She wants you, doesn't she?

And if she wants you, I hope she wants me, even if it's only until it's time for you to be born. I could use a little wanting, myself.

chapter THREE

*N*ora had thought she'd be all talk after dropping off Merrilee. There was certainly much to discuss, but Nora wanted to keep private her thoughts about the girl. She was an absolute enigma, but Nora felt drawn, uncertain whether it was because of the baby or Merrilee herself.

The girl was odd, a little different. Definitely rural and what some might deem unpolished, but in a warm, impressive way, like burnished copper. And she was polite, so much more so than most of the teenagers with whom Nora had been in contact. How many kids that age still said "yes, ma'am" and "yes, sir" like Merrilee?

Nora's mother would have said that Merrilee's mother raised her properly on at least one count. Manners were important to Mother, but if she were still living, she no doubt would have disapproved of Merrilee. Proper young girls didn't get pregnant.

Sometimes, neither did proper women, and Mother had died knowing that about her own daughter.

Back at the house, Steven leaned against the door from the garage and studied her. "Didn't you like Merrilee?"

"Yes, of course," Nora said, startled by the question. "Why do you ask?"

"You barely said three words once we left Chili's and nothing since we dropped her back at Adoption Lifeline."

Nora sank into the butter-soft, white leather sofa that overlooked the lake. Steven loosened his tie and sat on the bench of the Steinway angled in front of the tall windows. He looked down at the keys, but Nora knew he was watching her just the same, waiting in his own idle way. He launched into "Claire de lune," and Nora blinked. The piece always brought her deepest emotions to the surface.

"Was it difficult for you, Nora?" he said. "Seeing a pregnant woman, especially a teenager, must be."

"She's so young. Some of my friends have daughters her age."

"It's ironic that a girl can get pregnant so easily." His hands skimmed over the keys.

"Yes. But she seems very mature about it all. I think that's what worries me."

"That she'll change her mind?"

"I don't know. What do you think?"

Steven stopped playing and turned to face her. "I don't think she has a choice."

"But are we the couple she wants to raise her baby?"

"She said so. She said she wasn't going to change her mind."

"She's fifteen, Steven. Girls that age change their mind as frequently as their clothes."

"Not Merrilee. She's different. She's . . . ah, *headstrong* isn't the word I'd use."

"How about *determined?*"

Steven nodded. "That's more like it. I think she knows what she wants, and she goes after it."

"Or knows what she has to give up and is willing anyway," Nora said, speculating aloud. "But is she truly willing, Steven? That's the question. Maybe I'd believe her more if I didn't feel like she was holding back on us."

"I thought she was pretty up-front."

"I thought more of what she didn't say than what she did."

Steven frowned. "Do you think she's hiding something?"

"I'm not sure." Nora paused, trying to articulate what intuition had been whispering ever since dinner. "She seemed pretty unmoved about the baby's father dying. Was he just one in a string of sexual partners? Is she promiscuous?"

"Does it matter?"

Taken aback, Nora realized how much of her mother's attitude had been pressing in. The thought frightened her. "Why, no. It shouldn't. That just came out, Steven. What an awful thing for me to say."

He crossed his arms. "Is anything else that she didn't say bothering you?"

"I'd like to know what happened to her mother, even if it isn't our business to ask. I'd like to know how that affected her."

"Seems to me she would have talked about that if she wanted to."

Nora considered for a moment. "She was so direct about other issues—reading, an education—but when it came to questions about her future plans . . ."

"So she doesn't want to talk about herself."

"Still . . ." Nora trailed off and she looked away. The girl's reticence seemed amazingly mature, yet still, perhaps it was a cover. Maybe she'd checked out the Reys and found them lacking.

Or maybe it was just Nora herself who didn't measure up.

Steven sat beside her on the sofa and took her hand. "We have two months until the baby's born. Why don't you get to know her some more? Maybe you'll feel better."

Nora's voice came out small. "What if she doesn't want to spend time with me?"

"You won't know unless you ask, Blondie." Steven smiled. "You two don't have to bare your souls, but it'd be good to get acquainted. After all, you'll both be the mother of the baby, each in your own way."

"Oh, Steven, what am I supposed to do? Call her up and say, 'Hi there, Merrilee, let's bond'?"

"She probably just wants to be included a bit, Nora. To be seen as a person, not as a baby breeder. Why don't you meet on neutral ground? What do women like to do together?"

Relaxing, Nora grinned. "Look at men."

Steven patted her knee and rose. "You'll think of something."

"I'm glad you could meet me for shopping this afternoon, Merrilee," Nora said, keeping one eye on Highway 360 traffic and another on her passenger.

Merrilee stared straight ahead, her hand gripping the armrest. "Well, I wasn't doing much. Mrs. Pennywood said swimming's good exercise for me and the baby, so I went to the pool. But I don't swim very well. After that, there wasn't much to do but read."

"Oh? Reading anything in particular?"

Merrilee shrugged. "I picked through some old books Mrs. Pennywood has in the bookcases. I read a little bit of *Gone With the Wind,* but I got bored. I've read it five times already."

"I haven't read that book in years." Nora smiled in memory. "My mother took me to see the movie when I was about nine, and I was hooked. I probably read it five times before I was thirteen, myself."

"No kidding?" Merrilee's hand loosened from the armrest, and she turned toward Nora. "What else did you like to read when you were growing up?"

"The Little House on the Prairie books were probably my favorite. How about you?"

"Those were all right." Merrilee shrugged. "I like a little more adventure in my stories.

Something like Nancy Drew. I'm still on the lookout for a few I haven't yet read."

"You mean you know the titles?"

"I even know the numbers of the ones under a hundred," Merrilee said proudly. "Twenty-four, twenty-six, twenty-nine, thirty-two, thirty-seven, thirty-eight, thirty-nine, forty-one, forty—"

"You can remember all those numbers?" Nora couldn't believe the girl hadn't consulted a list. She knew grown women who could barely remember their own telephone numbers, much less such a mishmash of a sequence.

"Yep. I've been looking for them for so long, I got 'em memorized. There's twenty-six books in all, but like I said, those are just the numbers under a hundred. I have everything above that written in the back of my journal."

"You keep a diary?" Nora was charmed by the notion. She'd kept one, too, when she was nine years old.

"No, ma'am, not a diary. A journal. Seems to me like there's a difference, though I'm not sure how to explain it. A journal seems kind of more grown-up, somehow."

Nora deftly exited 360 and headed down a major street toward the tonier baby shops. "Lots of women pay good money to learn how to journal."

Merrilee shrugged. "I just write what I'm thinking about." She paused. "Actually, I wrote in it just for me the past year, but lately I've been writing in it for the baby."

"How sweet, Merrilee," Nora murmured. At the same time, she was struck with the notion that if only she could read the journal now, she might have a few insights into Merrilee Hunter.

Merrilee drew a deep breath. "I got to be honest, Miz Rey. I'm not sure if I'll be able to give up that journal. I mean, to the baby, after she's born."

"Why?"

Merrilee glanced out her side window. "There's a lot of stuff that's probably only meant for me and God to know. I write stuff for the baby, but by the time she's old enough to read it and understand what I'm saying, she probably won't want to know such things about her birth mama."

Nora held her breath. Merrilee hadn't indicated at their first meeting whether she wanted to stay in contact with them and the baby. Nora and Steven had agreed with Adoption Lifeline that they would abide by whatever decision any birth mother of their adopted child chose. Truly open adoptions were more commonplace, and while the thought of regularly sharing not only letters and photos but holiday visitations with a birth mother unnerved Nora, she was willing.

"She'll always wonder about you, Merrilee," Nora said. "She may ask you herself . . . if you choose to stay in contact."

Merrilee continued to stare out the window, and her words came out quiet but strong. "I don't see how I could."

Nora pulled into the parking lot of Chez Les Enfants and found a spot near the entrance. She shut off the engine and studied Merrilee, who was still looking out her window, twisting her hands in her lap. Nora could see the baby shift, and a mixture of jealousy and compassion raced through her. Compassion won out, and Nora concentrated on the fifteen-year-old girl sitting beside her.

"We don't have to shop for baby things," she said. *Clothes that you'll never get to see the baby wear. Blankets you'll never get to cover her with.* "I have to admit, I was surprised when you suggested that's what we shop for."

Merrilee shrugged. "Just seems natural. I sure can't afford anything for myself."

Nora studied her as they got out of the car. Was the girl fishing for presents? The adoption book warned that some birth mothers tried to get as much as they could from the adoptive parents. Merrilee hadn't struck her as a gold digger at their first meeting, but maybe now that she had Nora alone, her true colors would show.

The door chimed the opening line of "Frère Jacques" as they entered. Nora's heart lifted as she spied the beautiful, pristine baby clothes, toys, accessories—even the diaper pails. She hadn't been in the store for several years, and the last time she had, she'd left in tears at the thought of never being able to buy items for her own child.

Merrilee hung back, ducking her head.

"What's wrong?" Nora whispered.

"This place is really fancy," she whispered back, raising her eyes, then lowering them again. Nora followed her gaze to an expensively tailored saleswoman, who eyed Merrilee in her cutoff shorts, huarache sandals, and men's T-shirt with the sleeves chopped off at the shoulders. The saleswoman's face registered a mixture of amusement and dismay.

Nora felt her face burn. What difference did it make whether Merrilee was dressed in expensive maternity clothes or secondhand casual? She caught the saleswoman's eye and gave her a disapproving look of her own, then steered Merrilee toward the back, where the cribs and bedding were displayed.

Merrilee ran her hand over a bright-red chrome crib and gawked at the price tag. "Uh, do you and Steven have a bed for the baby yet?"

Nora nodded, her throat tightening. "I bought a crib about seven years ago. It was a really good sale, a beautiful crib." She paused. "We've never had a chance to assemble it."

"Oh," Merrilee said, looking embarrassed. "What does it look like?"

"Are you familiar with the Jenny Lind style?"

Merrilee shook her head.

"It's old-fashioned looking—curvy spindles all around the bed. Here, see? There's one just like it, although the one we have is white."

Merrilee moved to the Jenny Lind crib and stroked the top rail, smiling. "White would be pretty for a girl. This is a nice design. I kinda like old-fashioned-looking things for babies—not all this bright-colored stuff. That's more for kids who can run around and have fun. Babies need soft, quiet colors."

She touched the Mickey and Minnie Mouse mobile hanging above the crib and gave the music box a quick turn. "When You Wish upon a Star" sounded, and the characters danced above the empty bed. Merrilee blinked. "I really like lullabies. Have you bought one of these things yet?"

Moved by the emotion she read in Merrilee's eyes, Nora moved closer to the girl. "No, we haven't," she said. "What do you think the baby would like?"

Merrilee glanced away. "I don't know, Miz Rey. Seems like that's your call."

"Please call me Nora." She paused. "We can leave if you'd like, Merrilee. But if it's not too painful, I really would appreciate your opinion."

"Miz Rey . . . Nora," she amended, without looking up, "I told you and your husband that I'm not going to change my mind. You don't have to be nice to me because you're afraid I might."

"I'm not. Steven and I will accept whatever you decide. But if you choose us to raise your baby, I want you to have as much say as you desire. And that includes what the baby wears and what mobile she looks at." Nora hesitated. "If you want to help. But if it's painful—"

"It is." Merrilee drew a deep breath. "But

probably no more than it is for you. Coming to a baby store like this, I mean. It must have been hard to look at this stuff for all these years, knowing you couldn't have your own baby."

Nora marveled at Merrilee's perception. More than that, her compassion. Here she thought she'd been the noble one, and Merrilee was already thinking about her.

Neutral ground, Steven had said, for a meeting place. Be careful that the birth mother doesn't try to take financial advantage, the adoption book cautioned.

It seemed to Nora that she was the one taking advantage. She and Merrilee needed to explore their common ground, not find the neutral, like two generals discussing a truce.

Nora smiled. "What do you say we get out of here, Merrilee? The baby stuff can wait. Would you like to come to my house?"

"Are you sure you want me there, Miz Rey, uh, Nora? I know the book says you may not want me to know your address. In case I start bugging you guys after the baby's born or something."

"Why would I not want you to see where your baby's going to live? We can stop by your place and pick up your swimsuit and a change of clothes. Let's make a day of it. Steven's at work—it'll be just us girls." Nora studied Merrilee, who didn't respond. "You said yourself you didn't have anything to do. Besides, if you get tired of hanging with me, Steven and I have lots of books. Some of my old copies of Nancy Drew are on the shelves. I like a little adventure myself, some days."

Merrilee grinned bashfully. "Okay. It sounds like fun."

* * *

She's just interested in the baby. She's just interested in the baby.

Merrilee repeated the words all the way out to Nora's house. She tried to focus on the hills west of town, tried to soak in the memory of the scrubby terrain and cedars standing guard over shimmering Lake Travis. She wanted to tell Sylvie Ponds all about the scenery later, but she was too unnerved by the woman behind the wheel of the fancy Lincoln Navigator.

When they pulled into the driveway of the Reys' home, Merrilee was even more bowled over. "Wow," she said, licking her lips as the gate swung closed behind them and the large house loomed in front. "You guys must be really rich."

Nora parked the car in the garage, and Merrilee was out of the Navigator like buckshot, racing around the side of the house to check out the view. She clutched the paper bag holding her swimsuit and change of clothes.

They live on the lake! And a pool! Why would anyone have a pool when this gorgeous lake is right here? It's so—

A dog barked, and Merrilee pulled up just shy of the pool area. A large German shepherd bounded toward her, and she screamed. Dropping the bag, she hurried back toward the garage, her heart pounding madly. Barking louder, the dog gave chase. Merrilee's eyes filled with tears, and she ran straight into Nora Rey.

Nora put her arms around her. "It's all right, Merrilee. He's harmless. Really. Lucky! Down!"

Closing her eyes, Merrilee snuggled into

Nora's arms. The dog quieted, and Merrilee sensed that he had stopped a good distance away.

"Good boy," Nora said in an even, friendly tone. "This is Merrilee. She's my friend, and you scared her. I think you should apologize."

Merrilee opened her eyes. She couldn't believe this woman was talking to a dog like a person. She also couldn't believe she'd thrown herself at Nora Rey like a little kid. She peered around to make sure Lucky was still "down." The dog lay on the grass, looking up at her, panting . . . salivating . . . as though she were a choice piece of prime rib.

"There, you see?" Nora said to her. "He's really a nice dog. Just overly exuberant."

Merrilee eased away from Nora but stayed close. "Can we go into the house now? He stays outside, doesn't he?"

Nora laughed. "Most of the time. On an occasional stormy night, we let him in." She patted Merrilee's shoulder and then, as if realizing the intimacy of the action, cleared her throat. "Head for the front door. I'll get your bag and make sure Lucky has enough water; then I'll be right in. Here's the key."

Merrilee held the rest of the keys on the ring in the palm of her hand and held out the house key between her thumb and forefinger. What if she dropped the key ring and all the keys got mixed up? Nora had so many.

To her relief, she managed to get the door open. She quietly shut it behind her, catching her breath with a little gulp in her throat.

The house was gorgeous. Spotless. Beautiful. A wide-open "sittin' area," as Mama would have called it, with large, smooth ceramic floor tiles; deep, cushiony furniture and glass tables; several tall green, leafy plants in gleaming gold pots, bookcases filled with books; and a big black piano situated by the most wonderful view Merrilee had ever seen.

It was everything she'd ever want in a home, mostly because it overlooked the lake from tall glass panes. She could curl up by those windows in that rattan chair with the big cushion and dream the day away. She'd read a little, maybe sipping on some iced tea, then glance up from

her book and stare out those windows, watching
the world. Why, with a view like this, someone
could probably find a cure for all those termi-
nal diseases and create world peace! Someone
should fly in scientists and world leaders to this
very spot. All the answers in the world were
right out there, hovering over the lake, just
within reach, she was sure.

Merrilee shook her head. She'd have to
remember to write about this in the journal
tonight. To tell her baby that when she felt sad
or lonely or needed some answers, all she'd
have to do is sit by those windows and do some
praying. She could imagine her daughter sitting
there as a young girl with long hair, deep in
thought, worried over some childish thing.
Nora would kneel and put an arm around her.
"What's wrong, sweetheart?" she'd say. "What
can I help you with?"

Nora would be good at that. She'd be good as
a mother. Sympathetic. Maybe that's because
she liked to read. Mama hadn't been very good
at knowing when Merrilee was upset or hurting,
but then she hadn't ever gotten into books

much. She always said she was too busy living her life to stick her nose in some old book, the way Merrilee did.

Yes, it would be Nora Rey who comforted Merrilee's baby girl.

"Nora," she whispered to herself firmly.

"Goodness, Merrilee." Nora had opened the front door without Merrilee hearing. "Don't you want to sit down?"

"I was kind of afraid to. Everything's so nice."

Nora smiled, laying her purse on the kitchen counter, then setting Merrilee's paper bag beside it. "Have a seat, and I'll fix us some lemonade. Whew. It's like a steam bath outside." She fanned herself, and the loose blond hairs that framed her face rose up and fell back into perfect place. "You must be really hot, Merrilee. Let's have our lemonade; then we can go swimming."

"That sounds good." Merrilee glanced around the living room. "Can I sit anywhere?"

Nora smiled. "Anywhere you'd like."

Merrilee headed straight for the big-cushioned rattan chair by the window. It was tough to tuck her legs underneath her, cross-legged, but she finally managed. She felt like she was inside a cushioned bowl tilted sideways, secure and enclosed like the baby who danced inside her.

Merrilee glanced at the doorway and saw that Nora was still puttering in the kitchen. She put her hands on her belly and smiled. "It's a great place to sit, isn't it, Baby Girl? I wish you could see the view from my side of things. The lake's real blue and calm, and there're birds flying around out there on the rocks."

She glanced around the room. "If I was you, and I got tired of looking out these windows or reading all those books—though I don't think I ever could—I'd sit at that piano. I don't know how to play anything, but I'd sure learn. It's a beautiful piano, Baby Girl. Black and shiny. A grand piano, I think. Maybe a baby grand."

Merrilee rubbed her belly wistfully, and her voice dropped to a whisper. "A baby grand for a grand baby. I hope you learn how to play."

"Merrilee, wouldn't you like to sit over here?" Nora nodded at the plush L-shaped sectional sofa, then handed Merrilee a tall glass of lemonade. "It's much more comfortable than that old papasan chair."

"A *what* chair?"

"Papasan."

"Oh. Well, it's fine." She snuggled in. "Real cozy. Where'd you get it?"

Nora sat at the far end of the sofa. "It was the first piece of furniture Steven and I bought together, when we were newlyweds. It wasn't very expensive, but we had to buy it on time." She smiled, remembering. "Oh, how we dreaded those payments! I haven't had the heart to get rid of that chair, even though it's seldom used anymore. We keep it for sentimental value."

"Because you're doing so well now?" Merrilee felt her ears burn, and she sipped from the lemonade to cover her embarrassment. That was probably a rude thing to say. Mama said you shouldn't make mention of a person's money— whether he obviously had too little or plenty to spare.

The question didn't seem to bother Nora, though. "Having money isn't everything."

"It doesn't hurt." Merrilee glanced around the room.

Nora set her lemonade on the glass coffee table. "I don't keep the chair to remind us of how well we've done financially, but how we've overcome many struggles since those early days. Just like we knew we'd eventually pay off that chair, I've always believed we'll conquer all the obstacles that get thrown our way in marriage."

"Like not being able to have your own baby?" Merrilee immediately glanced down. "I didn't mean to blurt that out. I'm always talking without thinking."

Nora moved down the sofa, closer to Merrilee. "It's all right to mention it, Merrilee. Yes, one of our struggles has been my infertility."

"Oh."

Merrilee stared out over the water. Did Nora ever want to just get on a boat and ride away from shore, ride, ride, until she was far away from her problems?

Probably not. A woman like Nora probably coped well with her problems.

Still, Merrilee felt awkward sitting in this show house, awkward and fat and blessed in a way Nora would never be. It didn't seem right that she'd gotten a child the way she had, while Nora'd probably tried and tried for years with no success. She wanted to feel angry at her for wanting the one thing Merrilee herself wanted above all else, but all she could find in her heart was a desire to help.

"You're a very observant girl," Nora said. "I noticed that at the baby store. It was nice of you to think about my discomfort when that sales-woman was obviously giving you a negative once-over."

Merrilee shrugged. "I'm used to it, though I never really noticed it until it was obvious I was carrying a baby. Most of Palmwood treated me like that. They treated Mama that way too."

"What happened to your mother, Merrilee?"

Merrilee squirmed in the chair. She shouldn't have come here. She wished Nora had just showed her the baby's room and every place she'd be, then driven her back to the safety of Adoption Lifeline. People didn't ask questions there. Nora wasn't asking in a prying way, but she was asking all the same.

"If it's rude of me to have asked, don't feel you have to answer."

The trouble was, Merrilee didn't have the ability to lie. Mama'd raised her not to, even when it hurt to tell the truth.

"I don't guess it's rude of you to ask about Mama," she said slowly. "After all, you'll be raising her grandbaby." Merrilee felt tears at the back of her eyes, and she turned to the window. She was not going to blow it right here in the Reys' house, in this comfy chair, blow any chance for a good life for her baby. She turned back to Nora, steadying her voice. "Mama killed herself."

Nora's expression shifted from cool blandness to disbelief. "Oh, Merrilee—"

"It's okay." Merrilee drew a deep breath. *One, two, three . . . don't let her see.* "I've had about a month to get over it."

"A month isn't much time," Nora said gently, perching on the edge of the sofa. She looked like she wanted to say something, but instead, she clasped her hands together tightly.

"The time's gone by real fast." Merrilee drew another deep breath and smiled. "And now I'm here. Well, not like I'm living at your house or anything, but here in Austin."

The front door swung open, and Lucky bounded into the room. "Hey, Blondie!" Steven called. "Where ya hiding?"

Merrilee shrieked as Lucky headed straight for her. Tail wagging, he put his front paws on her knee. Merrilee cowered, arms protecting her face as she drew her legs up to protect the baby. "Shoo! Go away! Bad dog!"

"Lucky, down!" Nora said in sharp command. "Steven, come get Lucky."

"Merrilee!" Steven stopped short by the piano. "I didn't expect to see you here. Is Lucky bothering you?"

"Y-yes!" She hid her face in her arms.

"She doesn't like big dogs," Nora said, grasping Lucky's collar firmly. She gave the shepherd a stern look. "Especially big enthusiastic dogs."

Lucky ducked his head, as if he knew he was in trouble. He glanced at Merrilee and whined. Merrilee kept her face covered.

"I'll take him." Steven took him from Nora and headed outside.

Merrilee lowered her arms when she heard the door close.

"You're safe," Nora said, her voice sounding like a smile. "Is there any special reason you're afraid of big dogs?"

Another question. Nora Rey was pressing hard. Merrilee hesitated, then decided the story wasn't too revealing. "When I was little, one of my mama's boyfriends had a big dog—a Rott-weiler, I think it was. We never went to Mama's boyfriends' houses, but Mama said he owed her money and we'd had a lean week. She said he couldn't refuse her the money if he saw her little girl. We knocked politely on the door, but he didn't answer, even though his pickup truck was outside."

Merrilee shifted in the chair. "Then Mama pounded on the door, yelling 'bout how he owed her and did he want her little girl to starve. The door opened, and this big old dog came charging out, barking, teeth bared. He went for me 'cause I was smaller than Mama, I guess, and he tore a chunk of skin loose from between my eyes before Mama whacked him with her purse."

"What happened then, Merrilee?"

She shrugged. "All I remember is seeing blood and wondering if that old dog had ripped my eyes out, then the sound of a rifle shot and the man swearing up and down to my screaming Mama that he didn't mean us no harm and he'd pay for any medical bills."

She paused. "I got stitched up and we lived pretty good for a few weeks after that. We never saw that fellow again, though. Not long after, he moved away from Palmwood."

Nora cleared her throat. "I'm sorry about Lucky. He wouldn't hurt a fly, but I can see why you'd be afraid of him. I'll keep him away from you, Merrilee."

"Thanks."

"Feel like that swim now?"

Merrilee glanced out to the pool and saw Lucky chasing a bird. "Um, I don't think so."

Steven entered. "So, did you ladies find anything at the baby stores?"

Nora and Merrilee glanced at each other. "We didn't shop long," Nora said.

"Nora told me about the crib you have for the baby, though," Merrilee said, trying to make conversation. "It sounds pretty."

"Would you like to see it?" Nora said. "It's in the room we'll use as a nursery."

"Sure." Getting the conversation back to the baby made Merrilee feel on safer, firmer ground. She rose and followed Nora and Steven as they led the way down a carpeted hallway.

"We haven't decorated yet," Nora said, flipping on the room's light switch. "Right now it's still just a guest room."

Merrilee smiled. The room was light and airy, with wispy white curtains and furniture. Several watercolor paintings of old-fashioned-looking women and plump babies decorated the cream-colored walls.

"A friend of mine painted those," Nora said proudly. "She has five children, and each one was a model."

No wonder they're in the guest room. Nora's probably proud of her friend's work, but it must be an awful reminder that she can't have kids. "They're lovely," Merrilee said, wishing she'd never looked at them in the first place. The cherubic children made her feel not only bad for Nora but bad for herself as well. The women in the paintings probably had husbands in the background, as a real family should.

"Here we go." Steven lugged out the crib's four unassembled sides from a closet and held them out for inspection.

Nora blew on the dust, then wiped it with her hand, which came away grimy. "We'd take some soap and water to it before we set it up, of course," she said to Merrilee.

She nodded, touching the dirty rails with awe. *I'll never get to see you sleeping here, Baby Girl. But at least I know you'll have a nice bed.*

Nora cleared her throat lightly. "Thanks, Steven. Merrilee, I didn't mean to keep you so long. Are you ready to head back to Adoption Lifeline?"

Merrilee nodded, not sure of her voice, not sure of much of anything anymore.

chapter

FOUR

$\mathcal{N}$ora pulled the covers up to her shoulders and turned on her side, watching Steven brush his teeth in the bathroom just beyond their bedroom. He hummed while he rinsed the toothbrush, then washed his face.

Nora loved the strong curve of his bare shoulders, the trimness of his back as it disappeared into his pajama bottoms. Something as mundane as watching him lean over to splash water on his face still made her proud to be his wife after all these years. Would having a baby in the house change her feelings for him? Many of her friends had confided that children often changed a wife's perspective of her husband to a man who was the father of her children. She wasn't sure if this was a good change or not.

Nora rolled onto her back, squeezing her eyes shut. What had Merrilee thought about the father of her baby? She'd never expressed any affection for him, even though he was apparently dead. Had she loved him, in her own teenage way, as Nora loved Steven? Had she allowed him to take liberties in a vain attempt to keep him at her side?

The better she got to know Merrilee, the less inclined Nora was to think the girl promiscuous. Even though her mother sounded like she was seldom alone.

There you go again, Nora, making judgments. Just because the woman had a boyfriend or two doesn't mean she was a prostitute standing on the street corner.

Why had she killed herself? Oh, Merrilee!

"You've been quiet all evening again," Steven said. He flicked off the table lamp, plunging the room into moonlight. He slipped under the covers beside her.

Instantly she moved into his arms. "I've been thinking."

He kissed her below the ear, slowly. "And what's on Blondie's mind tonight? The baby?"

"Yes, a little. But I've been thinking more about Merrilee. Have you ever noticed that scar on the bridge of her nose?"

"Mmm hmm." Steven's kisses moved down her throat.

"She was attacked by a dog. That's why she's afraid of Lucky."

Steven eased his embrace, putting space between them. "What else did you learn?"

"Do you know how her mother died?" Nora's eyes filled with tears. "She killed herself, Steven. Imagine a girl that age, pregnant, unmarried, and her mother commits suicide. Then she brings herself here, to Austin, to let us adopt her baby."

"You'd never know from talking to her that she carried such burdens. She's more level-headed than most adults I know."

"Yes, but she—"

Nora broke off, remembering how Merrilee

had stared out their window, rubbing her belly. The maternal act had stopped Nora short in the kitchen, unwilling to intrude. She'd seen Merrilee's lips moving, as though she was speaking to the baby. Nora didn't think she'd ever seen love and compassion register so openly on someone's face, yet mixed with such impending sorrow. She'd realized then, watching Merrilee curled into the old papasan chair, that she and Steven would be taking from the girl that which she loved most.

"I want to help her, Steven," Nora said, pressing her cheek against her husband's bare chest. "She's so young, and she's all alone."

"We're going to help her by raising her baby."

"But then what happens to her? Is she going to go back to being a clerk at that small-town library, struggling to get her high school diploma? What kind of life will she lead? Who'll take care of her?"

"Probably the librarian—Miss Ponds, I think she said her name was."

"But what will Merrilee do with the rest of

her life? She's such an intelligent, compassionate girl, Steven. I can't let her just walk into our lives, place her baby in our arms, then let her walk away! Is that what God wants from us?"

Steven was silent for a moment. "Nora, you're getting too emotionally involved. I can't see that it's a good thing for you, Merrilee, or the baby. We agreed that we'd abide by whatever the birth mother wanted in terms of visits, letters, and involvement in the baby's life. But no one ever said anything about looking after her, too. Not even God."

He paused, then continued before she could speak. "Perhaps I was wrong in suggesting that you two get to know each other better."

Nora sat up. "Steven Rey, are you saying you don't care that her mother committed suicide just a month ago? that she's never known a father herself? How can you be so callous?"

"Of course I care, Nora." Steven laid his hand on her arm. "But I care more about you. And I don't want to see your heart broken yet again, like it has been every month, every year since we first decided to have children."

"You said if it was God's will that we have children, that we would," she said in a low voice. "You said to have faith. Everybody said to have faith—Father Thomas, our friends—everyone. And now it looks like we're finally going to get a baby. Who's going to have faith for Merrilee, Steven? Is she just supposed to swim upstream, spawn, then disappear from our lives? from our hearts?"

Her voice caught on a sob.

"Nora, Nora." Steven eased her back down beside him, into the comfort of his arms. "Shh. It'll be all right. Once the baby's born, it'll all work out. You'll see. We'll be busy with the baby, and Merrilee's life will go on. Have faith, Nora. It'll all work out."

Steven kissed her temples and cheeks. Nora closed her eyes and silently asked for such faith, asked for direction at this juncture of her and Merrilee's paths.

* * *

The next two weeks proved almost as nerve-racking to Nora as the multitude of preceding years during which she and Steven had tried to get pregnant. He convinced her not to contact Merrilee, to wait until they heard from her first.

"Mrs. Pennywood's told us she's fine. We've courted her, Nora," he said one morning at breakfast, when she wondered aloud why they hadn't heard from Merrilee herself. "We don't want to push the situation. We've made our desire for her baby clear."

"So has she," Nora said. "She assured us that she wasn't going to change her mind. What's the harm in spending time with her?"

"The harm might be to you if she does change her mind. The baby isn't ours until she signs the papers." Steven folded up the *Austin American-Statesman*. "Time for me to head to the office. How about you?"

Nora shook her head, swallowing from her coffee mug to hide the betraying expression certainly etched across her face. "I'm not handling any hot properties at the moment, so I'm not going in today. I have some things to do, errands to run, that sort of thing."

He kissed her and smiled as he headed for the garage. "I'll call later. Love you!"

"Love you too!"

The minute she heard the Lexus back out of the garage, she headed for her room to change clothes.

* * *

"I was surprised to hear from you, Nora," Merrilee said as they drove back toward the Rey home from Adoption Lifeline.

"Why is that?"

Merrilee shrugged. "I figured you'd met me and that'd be it. Until the baby's born, that is. Mrs. Pennywood says that's the way it is with most adoptive parents and birth mothers."

"She didn't advise you against meeting with me again, did she?"

Merrilee paused. "She said that if we're going to keep meeting, we should agree now on what's going to happen after the baby's born."

"You mean as to how involved you'll be in the baby's life?"

Merrilee nodded. "She said that if we don't

set the ground rules now, we could all be in for a lot of hurt later."

"Then we can discuss that when Steven gets home from work," Nora said, wondering how he was going to react when he found Merrilee at their home. "Meanwhile . . . I owe you a swim in our pool, remember? I'll put Lucky inside, and we can enjoy the outdoors. You brought your swimsuit?"

Merrilee nodded and held out a paper bag, identical to the one she'd brought before.

At the house, Nora ushered Merrilee to the guest room to change into her swimsuit. She changed quickly into her own suit, fingers trembling as she adjusted the straps.

Steven would be angry when he got home, but she wasn't going to sneak Merrilee in and out of the house. He just needed a chance to talk with her. Then he'd see that there was no reason to worry that the girl would cause them any pain. She was the mother of their child, after all. Until they could lavish their affection on the baby, didn't Merrilee deserve some attention too?

Merrilee was waiting out in the living room, looking nervous. Her stomach seemed even more pronounced, covered by the floppy blue maternity swimsuit. Long-lashed goldfish and much smaller baby goldfish playfully chased across the material.

"It's not exactly my style," Merrilee said, pointing at the suit, "but it's all Mrs. Penny-wood had to loan me."

"It's kind of cute, actually."

Merrilee shook her head. "Not like yours. Last summer I had a tie-dyed bikini and a great tan. Wayne said—" She broke off. "Well, that was last summer."

Nora was dying to know more, but she only smiled. "Let me put Lucky in the laundry room; then we can head outside."

"He'll be okay, won't he? I mean, it's not like a small space or anything, is it?"

"He'll be a little unhappy, but I set out some food and water and his favorite blanket in there. He'll curl right up and go to sleep."

Merrilee looked relieved.

Even though it was only the last week in May,

the sun's heat glared off the concrete around the pool. Nora slathered Merrilee's back with sunscreen, and the girl returned the favor.

"I hate this stuff, but I hate sunburn even worse," Merrilee said, working on her nose. "Once I got really sick from a bad sunburn. I wouldn't want to do that while I'm carrying this baby."

At that moment, the baby shifted vigorously, and Nora stopped her own sunscreen application, transfixed. "What does that feel like, Merrilee?"

"What? Oh, the baby?" Merrilee smiled. "Here. Feel for yourself."

She guided Nora's hand to her abdomen, and they were soon rewarded with another gymnastic maneuver. Nora laughed. "She's really thrashing around! She's like one of those fish on your swimsuit."

Merrilee laughed too. "That's what she feels like, all right. Like a big fish, whipping its tail around."

Nora withdrew her hand, smiling at Merrilee. "It must be wonderful when you can feel it inside you. You're so fortunate, Merrilee. So blessed."

Merrilee's smile faded. "Yeah, well, I don't know if *blessing* applies to all this. It's been more like a curse from my end of things. But the blessing is that you're going to get a baby after years of waiting, and my little girl will have a good home."

"What about you, Merrilee? What would it take to make you feel blessed?"

Merrilee looked out over the lake, considering. "I think," she said slowly, "if I could only go back in time about eight months."

"Before the baby was conceived?"

Merrilee nodded, then turned away. "Let's get in the pool. It's hot."

Another loose end. *Will I never know what's going on in that girl's head?*

Nora went straight to the deep end and dived in. When she surfaced, she saw that Merrilee was sitting on the pool steps, barely in the water.

"Come on in," Nora said, treading water at her end of the pool.

Merrilee shook her head. "I just like to get my feet wet."

Nora swam to the shallow end. "Can you swim at all?"

"Some. Not very well."

"You can float on your back, can't you?"

"I always sink. Especially now, with the baby."

"The extra weight won't matter in the water. Here, I'll help you. Stand up here, on the bottom of the pool."

Merrilee walked down the remaining steps to Nora.

"Now walk out a bit more, about up to your waist."

Merrilee grinned. "I don't have a waist anymore."

"Then where it used to be." Nora smiled back, walking backward until the water encircled her own middle.

Merrilee complied.

"Put your arms out, lean back on the water, and let your feet rise till you're lying on your back. Imagine that you're stretching out on a bed. You never worry about a bed collapsing under you, do you?"

Merrilee did as Nora asked, and Nora placed

her hands under Merrilee's back and knees, keeping her straight. Her stomach stuck up toward the sun.

"That's it, Merrilee. You can do it. That's it! Let the water hold you up. Now stay in this position."

Nora released her hands, and Merrilee stayed afloat. The girl grinned, waving her arms slowly through the water. She jumped upright, touched bottom, and flipped her wet hair back. Her smile lit up her face. "I did it!"

"Of course you did. You just needed a little help."

"I'm going to try it again."

Merrilee practiced floating while Nora swam laps. When her own stomach began to gnaw, Nora asked Merrilee if she was hungry, too.

"Starved!" said Merrilee happily, making her ungainly way up the pool steps. Water dripped in puddles around her.

"I'll bring lunch out here," Nora said. "Have a seat under the umbrella at the table. There are some towels there, too."

Nora brought out a tray of finger sandwiches

and vegetables with dip she'd prepared that morning, as well as plates and lemonade. Merrilee dug in with gusto but stopped after a few bites. "What kind of sandwich is this?"

"Cucumber. If you don't like it, you don't have to eat it. There're peanut butter sandwiches on the tray, too."

Merrilee chewed thoughtfully. "It's not bad." She chewed some more. "Pretty good, actually. Maybe you can show me how to make them. I like to fix new things."

"Do you like to cook?"

"Yes, ma'am. I cooked most of the meals for me and Mama since I was about ten years old. She worked at a café and hated the sight of food, so I figured I'd help her out some at home. Did most of the cleaning, too." Merrilee stopped, looking abashed.

"What's wrong?"

"I guess you're tired of hearing about me and Mama. Our lives must seem pretty inferior compared to yours."

"You think mine is better?" Nora was tired, all right. Tired of encountering the attitude that because she and Steven were rich they must think themselves better than others. Tired of the occasional subtle hints that they should regret having money, that it was somehow sinful.

Tired of people thinking that because they were wealthy, she didn't experience the same sorrows as everyone else.

"Yeah, I think your life is better. Look at this place. It's gorgeous. You've got a great husband, a job."

"Lives can't be measured by material possessions, Merrilee. That's not an indication of a person's success."

"No, probably not." Merrilee sipped her lemonade. "All I know is Mama wasn't a success by any long shot, and she certainly didn't have anything except our broken-down old trailer."

"You were probably her greatest treasure, Merrilee," Nora said softly. "She had you."

"Yeah." Merrilee smiled wryly. "She had me, all right. I used to think it was enough, just her and me, no matter how many men dumped her."

"Your mother had lots of boyfriends?"

Merrilee set down her lemonade. "Yeah. But they didn't stick around long. By the time I was nine, I knew they never would. But Mama kept on believing in that white knight who'd take care of us for the rest of our lives." She paused. "When this baby made her presence known, I figured it'd be enough to make Mama happy—me, her, and the baby."

"You were going to keep the baby?" Nora was intrigued by this revelation.

The girl nodded. "Mama's death changed everything."

"Merrilee, I want to understand." Nora leaned forward. "I don't want to pry, but you're, you're . . ."

"Holding back?"

Her choice of words, so self-helpish for a teenager, startled Nora. "Yes!"

Merrilee glanced down at her hands and said nothing.

Nora knew she should back off the conversation. Warning bells rang in her head that Steven was right—she was getting too emotionally involved. Part of her felt sorry for Merrilee, but part of her also resented that the girl seemed to hold all the trump cards in this adoption and wouldn't even admit that she did.

"Here. Have another cucumber sandwich." Nora passed the plate, giving in to defeat. At least for the time. Surely there was some way to break down Merrilee's guard, to gain her trust.

What surprised Nora was the realization that she cared, not so much because of the baby but because of Merrilee herself.

✳ ✳ ✳

Merrilee flat out loved the Reys' pool. It was clean and clear, unlike the public pool at Palmwood, which usually looked about as clear as the nearest creek, the one that ran downstream from the concrete plant.

But even as she perfected floating, Merrilee kept looking over her shoulder at the lake down the hill from the Reys' home. She felt greedy for wanting more, but it beckoned her, the sun glinting off the gentle waves, the bobbing buoys in the distance.

It was even better than the view from the Reys'
windows, everything so close and big, like when,
as a girl, she'd planted herself only two feet away
from the TV to watch.

"Merrilee, you're going to ruin your eyes, sitting that
close," Mama warned.

"No, I won't." Merrilee never took her eyes from
the screen. The black-and-white sitcom was riveting,
far removed from her life. "The eye doctor who came
to my school for exams said it didn't matter."

"Them doctors. What do they know, anyhow?"
Mama pulled deep on her cigarette, then tapped
the ashes into her empty beer glass. "Well, I guess
you're okay. Your teacher did send a note home
that your eyes are fine. But that don't mean you
can sit there all night. When Charley gets here,
you're going to have to turn off that contraption,
honey. I'll need you to play in your room for a
while."

"Oh, Mama, again? Charley's been over here
nearly every night this week. I can't watch any of my
favorite shows anymore!"

"Never mind, Merrilee," Mama said, waving her

cigarette. "He likes to come here and spend time with us—get away from that harpy he has for a wife."

"But Mama, I want to spend time with just you. Can't you tell him not to come over tonight? I won't even ask to watch TV—I promise! Maybe we could go get some ice cream or play a board game."

"Not tonight, Merrilee." Mama massaged her temples, as if she had one of her sick headaches. "Just remember that if we're good to Charley, he'll be good to us."

But he hadn't been, any more than any of them had been. Especially the last one, Lucas Procter.

And his son, Wayne.

"Merrilee? You keep staring at the lake," Nora said. "Would you like to walk down there?"

"Sure. It looks pretty from up here."

"There's a swing out at the boathouse, in the shade. If Steven were here, we could get him to take us for a boat ride. I don't much like to drive it, myself."

"I can't blame you. I started learning to drive

a car, and I'm not in a big hurry. I figure I'll just keep taking the bus around Palmwood. Leastways to places where I can't walk."

She rubbed at her back with a knotted fist. "It sure will be easier to do that when I'm not carrying this baby anymore. The doctor I saw said she wasn't a big baby, but she feels like a ton of bricks sometimes."

"Mrs. Pennywood said that the doctor thinks everything's fine. Did he say anything else to you?"

"Just to keep eating healthy. He scheduled one of those ultrasounds in two weeks." She ducked her head shyly. "Would you and Steven like to go with me?"

Nora smiled. "We'd be honored."

They walked down the tall stairway to the boathouse, Nora insisting on grabbing at Merrilee's arm every so often. "Are you sure you don't want to stop and rest?"

Merrilee grinned. "I'm fine, Nora."

"What about going back up? Will you be able to make it?"

"I guess women have been having babies and

walking up steps for a lot longer than I've been pregnant. I'll make it. Nothing'll happen to this baby."

"I'm concerned about you, too, Merrilee," Nora said.

Merrilee shrugged.

The boathouse was small, little more than a covered shed for waterskiing equipment and fishing tackle, but Merrilee thought it was grand. She wondered if the Reys would let her move in down here, where she could look out at the lake every day and keep an eye on her baby, growing up there on the hill above.

Dejected, she slumped down on a double-seater redwood swing, attached to the roof's overhang with heavy chains. If she swung high and fast enough, she could launch herself out over the water into a crazy dive. The idea cheered her a little; then she remembered that she'd better resist temptation for the baby's sake.

Nora sat beside her, and Merrilee stiffened. She liked the woman a lot, the way she liked Sylvie Ponds, but unlike Sylvie, Nora persisted with gentle questions that threatened Merrilee's defenses. Sylvie never asked anything. Merrilee was grateful for the privacy, but she sometimes wondered if maybe Sylvie just didn't have enough sense to realize what had happened. Apparently nobody in Palmwood did, which accounted for the cold shoulders she'd gotten since her pregnancy had become obvious.

Especially since Mama died.

Merrilee studied a hummingbird feeder hanging at the edge of the roof. Two birds zipped in and out, their wings fluttering too quickly to be seen.

"Is your mama still alive?" Merrilee said abruptly. "Will my baby have grandparents?"

"Steven's parents live in Massachusetts. We visit each other at least twice a year. Steven's brother and sister each have two children, so his folks are experts at grandparenting. They're good at it, too. Just enough spoiling to make a child feel special, and plenty of good, solid loving."

Merrilee kicked her feet against the rough boards of the boathouse pier to set the swing in motion. "What about you?"

Nora absentmindedly set her end of the swing in rhythm with Merrilee, shading her eyes against the sun. "They're both dead. My father died when I was a teenager. My mother died just a few years ago."

"What of?"

"She had a stroke. It was a blessing, really, that she passed on."

Merrilee squinted. "Why would you say that?"

"The stroke incapacitated her. She couldn't speak, couldn't move one side of her body, even. She had to be spoon-fed her meals."

"At least she was still alive."

Nora pressed her feet against the pier, slowing the swing's motion. "My mother was a huge perfectionist, Merrilee. Everything had to be perfect, just right, or life wasn't worth living."

Merrilee sat, thoughtful. "Must have been hard on you, though, when she passed. You have any brothers or sisters?"

Nora shook her head. "No, she just had me to ride herd on for my whole life."

Merrilee laughed. "Ride herd on you? No way! I bet you were the perfect kid."

"I tried, but it was never enough." Nora paused. "Even my not being able to get pregnant was a black mark against me."

"But you couldn't help that."

"I wish I'd been able to convince Mother of that. She wanted grandchildren so much. Not to play with and love, like most grandmothers, but as showpieces. To prove that her daughter, Nora Templett Rey, wife of the stellar orthopedic surgeon, Steven Payne Rey, could perform the most basic biological feat—to be fertile."

"I think my mama was just the opposite," Merrilee said. "She didn't think I'd ever get pregnant."

"Was she angry when you told her? Did she know early on?"

Merrilee looked Nora dead in the eye. She wanted to say, "Stop pressing!" It hurt to talk this much, not because of what she was afraid she might reveal but because of what she was afraid she wouldn't. Nora was actually interested—seemingly not for gossip's sake but out of concern.

Concern for the baby, of course, you dunderhead. She

*wants to make sure Mama didn't beat me or anything, to
cause any damage.*

"She wasn't angry so much as disappointed,"
Merrilee said. "She knew better than anybody
that single moms have it bad."

> *Mama just stared after Merrilee announced she'd
> taken a home pregnancy test that came out positive.
> "Didn't you tell the boy to use something, Merrilee?"
> she said, shaking her head. She lit a cigarette and
> stared out the small, smudged window of the trailer's
> kitchen. "You told Wayne yet?"*
>
> *"No, ma'am," she whispered. "I think he's moved
> out of town, anyway."*
>
> *"You think?" Mama turned, her eyes liquid fire.
> "You chose to get cozy enough with a boy to be carry-
> ing his seed and you don't know where he is?"*
>
> *"I haven't seen him in a fistful of weeks, Mama.
> Haven't you noticed he stopped coming around?"*

Haven't you noticed that I'm glad,
Mama? Haven't you noticed that I've
been crying into my pillow every night?
Didn't you even see that I was throwing
up every morning? You probably could

have told me what was wrong long before this cheap drugstore test!

"His daddy ain't been coming around neither," Mama said bitterly, squashing the cigarette in the sink. Her eyes spit fire at Merrilee. *"You reckon Lucas heard about this baby you got yourself with and told his boy to stay away? Then took his own advice and is staying away from me, too?"*

"I don't know, Mama," Merrilee said, misery welling up inside her. *"I don't care about the Procters."*

Mama gripped her arm, hard. *"Merrilee, you ain't a little girl anymore that I can hold in my lap and sing sweet little songs to. But now you got yourself in this fix, and I suppose you want me to help you out. Well, you know I can't abide by no abortion, so I reckon you'll have to have this kid. But you're going to have to go to work, same as me, to contribute."* She released her arm with a shove. *"So just forget about school and go get yourself a job. We'd better start saving our money for diapers and such. Babies cost money."*

"What about adoption, Mama?" Merrilee said, her lip trembling.

Mama stared. "Girl, this is your cross to shoulder. Not some puppy you go palming off on others. Leastwise, that's what my mama told me when I got pregnant with you." She pushed the cigarette stub in the disposal and ground the blades. "The pity of it is that you're making me shoulder this cross too."

"Your mother wanted to keep the baby?" Nora said. "For you and her to raise together?"

Merrilee rose, turning to face the house, away from Nora's probing eyes. "She was willing." She cleared her throat. "You and Steven—you're churchgoers, right?"

"Yes. We're members of a large Episcopalian church."

Merrilee didn't know anything about Episcopalians, outside of some folks at Gospel Fellowship referring to them as "stiff-necked tradition lovers." "But you pray and . . . and believe in Jesus?"

"Yes." Nora smiled. "How about you, Merrilee?"

"Oh, yes, ma'am. I believe in him. That's why

it's important that my baby be raised by Christians."

"Nora! Nora!"

Steven bounded down the steps, followed by Lucky, who barked cheerfully, running ahead of his master. Merrilee panicked and scrambled behind the swing, squatting to protect herself.

"Steven! Merrilee, it's all right. I'll take Lucky up to the—"

"Merrilee?" Steven ran the last of the distance and gripped Lucky by the collar to hold the dog back. His face was puzzled. "What are you doing here?"

Merrilee rose. "Nora invited me." She edged around the swing, using it now for protection, not from Lucky but from being seen by Steven. She felt uneasy in her swimsuit, stomach sticking out to there, her legs and arms all exposed.

Nora seemed to sense her discomfort and handed her a towel from the shed. "We've had a lovely time today, Steven. I was going to ask Merrilee to stay for dinner, if she'd like, so that we can discuss the baby."

Steven raised an eyebrow at his wife, and Merrilee instinctively realized all wasn't well between the couple. She knotted the towel around herself and edged toward the stairway. "I probably better be getting back. We can talk another—"

"No, stay, Merrilee," Steven said. He shot Nora a questioning look; she returned it with a gentle smile. His face relaxed and he smiled, then turned to Merrilee, the tension gone. "As long as you're here, this would be a good chance to talk."

Merrilee glanced between husband and wife and decided all was safe. Whatever argument they'd been nursing had passed between them and flitted away like one of the hummingbirds at the feeder. She'd never seen such a quick end to a disagreement between Mama and any of her male friends. Not one.

She smiled inwardly and touched her belly as she headed up the stairs with Steven and Nora behind her, each with an arm wrapped around the other, Lucky in tow.

After putting Lucky back in the laundry room, Nora hastily thawed thick steaks. She watched from the window as Steven fired up the outdoor grill and heard Merrilee laugh when he donned his customary white chef's hat and apron. Nora smiled as she stood at the sink and rinsed baking potatoes. After popping them into the oven, she joined Steven and Merrilee outside.

Hearing her leave the house, Lucky barked and scratched the door.

"Are you sure he's okay?" Merrilee said, a worried expression on her face. "I'm sorry he needs to be penned up."

"It's all right, Merrilee. He's fine." Nora said. She smiled at her husband. "I see Merrilee feels the same way about your barbecuing getup as I do."

"It's my good-luck outfit," Steven said to Merrilee. "If I don't wear it, the steaks burn."

"Merrilee, would you like to go have a long, warm bath while dinner cooks?" Nora said. "This'll take a while."

"That would feel good. I like swimming, but the chlorine always makes me itchy. Not that there's anything wrong with your pool," she added hastily.

Nora smiled and took her arm. "Come on. I'll show you to the guest bath."

When Merrilee was happily ensconced in the marble garden tub with the built-in whirlpool, Nora rejoined Steven outside. She put her hand on his arm. "Thank you for asking her to stay."

Steven set down the turning fork. "You've already decided how you want to handle this, Nora. All I can do is back you. She is a nice girl, and perhaps I should take the chance to know her better myself."

"But . . ."

He turned back to the grill. "Let's see what she has to say tonight about her future with the baby, once we become the parents."

"Would it be so terrible if she wanted to stay involved?"

"No." He kissed the tip of her nose.

"It would give her some stability, Steven. A place to go, people who cared about her."

Steven studied her thoughtfully. "You do care about her, don't you? Pretty deeply, too."

Nora nodded. "I want her to stay involved, Steven. I want to look out for her."

"Nora . . ."

"I have to believe God put this love for her in my heart, because I prayed about being involved with her. I know she can still decide to keep the baby. But I don't believe she will. I don't believe either of them will leave our lives."

"We'll see. We have a few more weeks to find out."

* * *

"Dinner was wonderful, Nora. Great steaks, Dr. Rey." Merrilee smiled, then realized how much the effort hurt. A dull throb built at the back of her neck and spread upward.

"Call me Steven." He smiled at Merrilee over the empty dessert plates that Nora began to clear from the table. "Did you get enough to eat?"

Merrilee patted her belly. She felt like she was carrying twins. "More'n enough. I don't think this baby and I need to eat for about two weeks."

Steven cleared his throat. "Maybe this would be a good time to talk about him—"

"Her. It's a girl, Dr., er, Steven. I'm sure of it."

"I think she's right," Nora said, smiling at her husband as she rejoined them at the table. "Merrilee seems to be in good touch with this baby." She took Steven's hand and smiled broadly. "We'd better plan on a girl."

Steven looked uncomfortably at Nora, then at Merrilee. "Anyway . . . I think it's time we talk about your plans for involvement after the baby's born."

"I think it's best I not be involved at all," she said. The dull throb was building into a dull roar in her brain, and she struggled to keep track of the conversation. "If I didn't think the baby'd be interested in her biological parents someday, I wouldn't even have my name on the birth certificate. But I don't want to make it difficult for her later if she has questions or anything."

"We're willing for you to be involved in the baby's life," Nora said. "In fact, we'd welcome it."

Merrilee shook her head, swallowing the burning tears in her throat. Why did they have to talk about this? "No, ma'am. It wouldn't be right. I don't want her confused while she's growing up. She'll just need one mommy . . . and a daddy. And you two will be it."

"You have until the baby's born—even after—to change your mind," Steven said.

"No, sir, I won't. This is what's best for everybody, especially her."

"But, Merrilee—"

She couldn't bear to see the stricken expression on Nora's face. Couldn't she understand that what she asked was too much for Merrilee to give? Wasn't it enough that Merrilee was entrusting them with her baby? Did they want her, too?

Her head filled with a sound like a swarm of bees, buzzing and stinging. Maybe this was what Mama's sick headaches had felt like, what her whole life had felt like.

Maybe the day she'd died, she just couldn't take the noise anymore and chose the best solution she could manage.

"Can I go sit on your sofa for a while?" Merrilee said. "My head hurts something awful." Her vision was getting dim from the headache, and the hum inside her head intensified.

Steven guided her to the sofa, and she sat down. Nora fussed over her, putting her feet up so that she was lying down.

"Probably too much sun," she heard Steven say.

Someone draped a light blanket over her, then tucked her in. "Sleep well, Merrilee," Nora whispered softly, then kissed her forehead.

Merrilee sighed and curled into the blanket, instinctively curving one arm securely around her belly.

✳ ✳ ✳

When she awoke, the room was pitch-black, save for the dim light of the moon shining through the windows. Merrilee sat up, grateful to find her headache diminished.

The kitchen microwave clock read four

o'clock. Merrilee groaned, knowing Mrs. Pennywood would worry. Maybe even now the state troopers were out looking for her. Mrs. Pennywood had strict rules about curfew. Other girls had tested her on it, just for the sake of being contentious, but Mrs. Pennywood had a way of making them regret it by giving them extra homework after schooltime.

Merrilee heard a sharp whine from the laundry room, and she started. Then she remembered Lucky was inside, and she moved through the kitchen and cautiously approached the door. "Are you okay?" she whispered.

Lucky scratched the door and whined louder.

Merrilee bit her lip. What if he'd run out of food and water? What if he needed to go outside to go to the bathroom? She wouldn't care for being penned up if she were in similar straits.

"If I let you out, will you give me a head start so that I can run for the bathroom to close the door? Maybe you'll go find Nora and Steven, huh? I bet you know where their bedroom is. They'll let you outside."

Lucky whined once more, then abruptly stopped.

Merrilee's heart pounded. "Lucky?" She edged open the door, ready to make a run for it.

Lucky sat on his haunches, polite as a show dog. His tail swish-swished against the floor at the sight of her, but otherwise, he remained motionless.

"Well, I'll be." Merrilee pushed the door completely open.

Lucky remained in a sit-stay position. He whined, then panted.

"Good boy. That's a good boy," Merrilee crooned, slowly extending her hand. When he didn't move, she touched his head lightly, and when he still didn't move, she stroked him between the ears. "Why, you're just a big old pussycat!"

"Nora says that's what he thinks he is."

Merrilee turned. Steven stood at the other end of the kitchen, his hands jammed into the pockets of his bathrobe. Lucky yelped and scurried toward him, winding himself around his legs.

"I hope Lucky and I didn't wake you up," she said.

"Not at all." Yawning, Steven moved to the counter and removed the carafe from the coffeemaker. "I always get up this early. Gives me a chance to think. Sometimes I go for a jog."

"I guess you'll be getting up this early a lot with the baby," Merrilee said, trying to joke. Without Lucky to pet anymore, she felt vulnerable.

"I'm sure I will." Steven smiled, coffee scoop poised over the filtered basket. "Do you want some of this?"

"No thanks."

"Oh, that's right. Sorry. It's not good for the baby."

"I never liked it much, anyway, though I used to drink it sometimes at night to keep myself awake until Mama got home from work."

"Where did she work?"

"At a little café in Palmwood. She was the lead waitress for as long as I can remember, and whenever anybody was sick, she had to take their shift. Since the place was open from 6:00 A.M. to midnight, she could make good money."

"Who stayed with you when she was gone?" Steven flipped the coffeemaker's On switch.

"Nobody." Merrilee shrugged. "From about the time I was in first grade, I could take care of myself."

Steven studied her a moment, then opened the refrigerator door. "Would you like a glass of milk?"

"Sure." Merrilee took a seat at the table. Lucky sat beside her, then curled up at her feet. Merrilee smiled and reached down to pet him.

Steven brought her milk and his coffee to the table. "I hope you don't mind skim milk—that's all we have."

"I don't mind at all," she said, lying. To her way of thinking, it tasted more like water. She drank it anyway and at least found it good and cold.

"How's your headache?"

"Much better." She drained the glass and wiped her mouth with the back of her hand.

Embarrassed that Steven had caught her in the action, she lowered both hands to her lap.

Steven smiled, as if he realized her embarrassment and wanted to put her at ease. "You and I haven't had a chance to talk alone, and there's something I've wanted to ask you."

"Wh-what?" She could think of a million questions she didn't want to answer.

"I know you grew up without a father, so I imagine you're more than qualified to give me some ideas on what would make a good dad."

Merrilee silently let out a whoosh of relief. "That's easy enough."

"Really?" He raised an eyebrow.

"Sure. You love your kids no matter what they do or what happens to them."

"That's it?"

What kind of answer had he expected? "Yeah, that's it." She paused. "I've been reading the Bible since I was about eleven. And the more I read it, the more I see that message. If we belong to God—if we're his kids—he loves us no matter what." She was clinging to that belief now, even though lots of folks—and her own head, at times—had told her otherwise for months. But God knew the truth and loved her even more than she loved this baby.

"Do you believe that kind of love is possible for mortals?"

"What do *you* believe?" Merrilee drew a shallow breath and held it.

"I believe that it's only possible by faith . . . and God's grace."

Merrilee quietly exhaled. "I want my baby to be raised with that. I want her to have a Christian family."

"Nora and I are believers," Steven said.

Merrilee nodded. "That's what she said. I'm glad to hear you say it, too. Only someone who understands God's love can give it in return. Just make sure that, even if you're really angry at my baby about something she's done, you let her know you love her anyway. Sometimes—" She faltered, the memory of Mama intruding. Her voice dropped. "Sometimes you find out later you were wrong about everything."

Steven took her hand. "Merrilee, would it

surprise you if I said you seem to understand unconditional love better than anybody I know?"

She nodded.

"I don't know anybody else who has your unconditional love for a child. I'll do my best to always remember that love and sacrifice, and match it with my own."

"You're going to be a great dad." She eased her hand from his. Such talk made her uncomfortable. "Nora said you two would come with me for my ultrasound in two weeks . . . did she mention it?"

"Only about a hundred times last night. It's nice of you to ask us."

"I'll be happier with you there. I don't much like doctors' offices." Then, remembering he was a doctor himself, she hastily added, "You never know what's going to happen there."

Steven laughed. "I have lots of patients who think exactly the same way. Some of them are so nervous, they have to be pulled down from the waiting room walls. Me, I'm not keen on going to the dentist's office."

"Ha! That's nothing bad. All he does is check your teeth. Or maybe fill a cavity."

"The sound of the drill doesn't bother you?"

"Nope." Merrilee rose, yawning. "Maybe you'd better take me back to Adoption Lifeline. Mrs. Pennywood will be worried."

"We phoned her last night and let her know you were staying with us. Why don't you go back to sleep for a while? Nora can drive you back later in the morning."

She yawned again. "A little more sleep does sound good."

"Great." Steven smiled. "Thanks for chatting with me, Merrilee. I'm glad you spent some time with us."

"Me too. Good night. Again."

She headed back to the couch, Lucky padding alongside her. Merrilee covered up, and Lucky plopped down on the floor beside her. "You're a good dog," Merrilee whispered, patting his head. She curled up under the blanket, secure and happy.

✳ ✳ ✳

Dear Baby Girl,

Now I know for sure you're going to have a great dad. Don't let a day go by without reminding yourself how fortunate you are to be with him.

Lucky's a nice dog too. You and he are going to be pals.

chapter

FIVE

The next two weeks reminded Merrilee later of the square of baking chocolate she'd bit into as a little girl: so appetizing to look at, so tasty at first bite, then acrid on the tongue. Time became bittersweet—an oxymoron, as her English teacher would have explained the literary term. When she wasn't attending Adoption Lifeline's school or doing chores around the maternity home, Merrilee spent most of her free time with the Reys.

Steven and Nora took her boating on the lake, and she watched Nora ski. When Merrilee said that it looked like fun and she'd love to try it—except for the baby—she could see in Steven's eyes that he wanted to say, "You can, after the baby's born." Instead, he turned away. He knew as well as she that their friendship would soon end. As much as she wanted to become a part of their lives, she knew that she couldn't.

Nora was the only one who acted as if nothing would change. Against her better judgment, Merrilee allowed herself to shop with Nora for baby things—blankets, sheets, designer clothes as well as more practical sleepers and onesies. Nora even purchased a lacy white outfit and said that she thought it would make the perfect christening gown. Merrilee said she thought it would, too, then silently reminded herself she wouldn't be around to see the baby wear it.

She wanted to stay away from the Reys. Each time they called—or she found herself picking up the phone because she was lonely and needed to chat—she told herself it would be the last time. Then she would have so much fun with them, feel so loved and wanted, that she couldn't stop from thinking about their next meeting.

While Merrilee admired the home, cars, and boat, she realized that it wasn't that their material possessions brought out any envy in her. No, it was that the love Steven and Nora consistently regenerated between themselves spread outward to include her.

She missed Mama's loving. As time grew closer for her own baby's birth, she found herself wishing she could crawl up in Mama's lap once again and be comforted herself.

The day before the scheduled ultrasound, Mrs. Pennywood called Merrilee into her office, then shut the door for privacy. "Merrilee, I'm worried about you," she said, without fanfare.

"Why? The doctor said everything seems good. And tomorrow we'll—"

Mrs. Pennywood shook her head. "Not the baby. I'm worried about your emotional state. I would never try to influence you one way or another about signing the adoption release papers, but I'm concerned that your continued involvement with the Reys will make a final decision more difficult for you."

Merrilee lifted her chin. "I told you, I told them, that I'm signing those papers. I want them to raise my baby. Why would spending time with them change my mind?"

"Because the parting will be so much more difficult. Having a baby is emotional enough. After the delivery, you may not be thinking clearly about what's best for the baby. You may only be thinking about how much greater your losses will be—losing not only the baby but the Reys as well. And so you might decide to keep the baby."

"I won't." Merrilee clenched her teeth. Why wouldn't anybody believe her? How could she explain that deep in her heart she knew this was what God wanted, no matter how much it hurt? Surely he would give her the strength, just as he had always fortified her in the past. Hadn't she always prayed that he would?

Even her prayers for herself continually led back to God's answer for her baby's future. No matter how much she already ached with loneliness, Merrilee couldn't raise her baby by herself. Alone, she couldn't give her daughter the kind of life she needed, something far removed from Palmwood.

That night Merrilee lay in bed, wishing she had the strength to get up and write in the journal. She hadn't written much in the past two weeks, since she'd started spending so much time with the Reys. A wave of guilt washed through her, as if she were being disloyal. Every day she was squandering her last few chances to talk to the baby. In scarcely a month, she'd be out of opportunities.

"I'll be back in Palmwood, and you'll still be here in Austin," she whispered, laying her hands on her belly. She would miss the giant curve of her stomach, would miss the physical touch. At times she almost felt as though her Baby Girl was pressing her tiny hands against her own—their own private, silent communication.

Tonight, however, the baby was quiet and still.

"I'll see you tomorrow," Merrilee whispered.

"Really see you—well, at least an image of you—on the sonogram machine. Then in about a month, we can meet face-to-face, okay, Baby Girl?"

Merrilee pressed her hands against her belly. The baby didn't respond.

"All right, then," Merrilee said, disappointed. She yawned and rolled uncomfortably to her side. "Sleep tight."

✳ ✳ ✳

"Steven, please hurry!" Nora called to her husband while she fussed with an earring. "We don't want to be late."

"We've got plenty of time," he said, but even he looked nervous as he straightened his tie with one hand and grabbed his car keys with another.

The drive into town seemed interminable. Nora chewed her lipstick off twice, a nervous habit she'd thought long kicked. *Hurry, hurry,* she sang inwardly. *We're going to see the baby today! Oh, hurry, hurry.*

"What if it's a boy?" Steven said. "Do you think Merrilee will be disappointed?"

"Probably. She's completely convinced this is a girl." Nora sighed happily. "I can't believe we're going to find out today. We're going to see our baby, Steven! Can you believe it?"

Steven considered for a moment. "We need to be careful of Merrilee's feelings during the ultrasound today."

"I know." Nora sobered. She wouldn't hurt Merrilee's feelings for anything in the world.

"More than that, we need to remember that Merrilee's a tangle of emotions, anyway. Being on the verge of saying good-bye to her child makes her doubly vulnerable to sadness. And Mrs. Pennywood says we can expect more signs of grief in these last few weeks before delivery. She said Merrilee might even refuse to see us."

"She wouldn't do that . . . would she?"

Steven shrugged. "Unless I miss my guess, what Mrs. Pennywood's trying to say in her delicate fashion is that maternal love is waging serious war with Merrilee right now. And we may come out on the losing side."

"With no baby?"

"That's one scenario. Another is an abrupt

closure to our friendship with Merrilee. You can't expect her to simply say it's been fun, thanks for the good times, then blithely walk away."

Nora felt torn. She understood what Steven was saying, but she didn't know how to think beyond the inevitable farewell, didn't know how to make things better for any of them.

She would miss Merrilee, too. More, she was certain, than she even realized in this moment of joy.

* * *

Merrilee was already lying on an examining table, dressed in a paper gown, a paper sheet pulled up to her stomach. Tension reflected in her eyes, like a cornered wild animal. She glanced at the bank of high-tech machinery to the side of the table, then at Nora. She extended the hand closest to the machinery as if she were pleading for a stay, and Nora took it between her own. Merrilee's skin was cold and clammy.

"I'm scared," she whispered.

"It won't hurt," Nora said. "They're just going to run a little microphone-looking thing over your tummy."

"I'm still scared." Merrilee gripped her hand tighter. "Where's Steven?"

"He's parking the car in the garage. I wish you'd have let us pick you up."

"Mrs. Pennywood was going to visit a friend in the hospital, and since the doctor's office is just next door—"

The door swung open, and a woman in pastel scrubs entered, a chart in her hand, all smiles. "Hi, Merrilee. I'm Barbara, and I'll be helping you take a look at your baby today."

"Hi," Merrilee said in a small voice.

Barbara took a seat at the machinery and busied herself with preparations. "I'm glad to see you brought your mom along, Merrilee."

Nora frowned. "I'm not her mother; I'm—"

"She's my friend," Merrilee cut in. "Her name is Nora. Nora Rey. And her husband, Steven, will be here in a moment. I asked them to be here."

Barbara glanced at the chart, then took a

longer look. "Oh." She read a bit more, then smiled again at Merrilee. This time her expression was more compassionate than chipper. "I understand, honey. Mrs. Rey, if you'll stand on the other side of the table, we'll get started."

Nora complied as Barbara turned the monitor toward them and punched a few buttons and dials. Merrilee drew a deep breath and smiled at Nora, then turned her attention to the monitor. Nora took her hand again and instinctively smoothed back Merrilee's hair.

I haven't prayed enough for her. She's so young to be lying on that table. She's still just a girl herself.

"This is warm gel, Merrilee," Barbara said, holding up a squeeze bottle. "I have to put it on your abdomen so the transducer can make good contact, all right?"

Merrilee nodded, biting her lip.

Barbara lifted the paper gown and lowered the sheet just enough to expose Merrilee's rounded belly. She squirted gel, and Merrilee flinched, laughing. "That *is* warm."

Barbara smiled. "Can you see the monitor? How about you, Mrs. Rey?"

"Yes, just fine," Nora said. Where was Steven? He was going to miss everything!

Barbara touched the tip of the transducer to Merrilee and rolled it around until a shadowy image appeared. "There's your baby's feet, Merrilee," she said. "See that there? She's a smart girl—head down, just like she's supposed to be. And there's her little rump. . . ."

"What're all those white lines?" Nora said, her voice catching in her throat.

"Those are bones. There's a leg . . . here's her pelvis. . . ."

"It's really a girl?" Merrilee whispered.

Barbara grinned. "She sure is. See right here? That's where we look. And farther up here are her ribs and—"

Barbara broke off, her brows furrowing as she rolled the transducer across Merrilee's skin.

"I thought maybe you could tell it was a girl by an extra rib," Nora said, laughing, then smiled down at Merrilee. "Remember the story of God taking a rib from Adam so that he could make woman?"

"We don't have to worry about names for boys

anymore," Merrilee said, smiling at Nora. "Now all we have to do is come up with a girl's name."

Barbara abruptly swiveled the monitor away from their view, still working the transducer.

"Is something wrong?" Nora said. Merrilee gripped her hand, silent.

Barbara glanced up, her eyes sorrowful. "Dr. Welch will want to have a look, ladies. Excuse me."

She all but sprinted for the door, passing Steven without speaking.

He turned to them for explanation. "Did she forget something?"

Nora wanted to move to him for comfort, but that would mean letting go of Merrilee's hand. "We saw the baby, Steven; then she turned the monitor away. Like she didn't want us to see. She's gone to get the doctor."

"I'm sure he wants to have a look for himself," Steven said, moving to Merrilee's side. "How ya doing, kiddo?"

"I . . . I'm not sure."

The door opened, and Steven moved beside

Nora while the doctor entered. He nodded curtly at them, then, without speaking, held a stethoscope to Merrilee's abdomen. He listened intently, then moved the stethoscope several times. He nodded at Barbara, who handed him the transducer. Like her, he rolled it over the goo on Merrilee's stomach and studied the monitor.

At last he exchanged a glance with Barbara and nodded once. He laid down the transducer, and Barbara quietly left the room, her head bowed.

Nora felt faint, but she had to hold on to Merrilee's hand. Steven braced up against her and laid one hand on Merrilee's shoulder and the other on Nora's.

Merrilee lay still and quiet.

"There's no easy way to say this," the doctor said, looking first at Merrilee, then at the Reys, then back to Merrilee. "But the baby's dead."

"No!" Nora startled herself by the vehemence in her voice.

Steven gripped her shoulder. "Are you sure? Aren't there more tests you can run?"

"Merrilee, has the baby been still lately?" Dr. Welch said. "When's the last time you remember him moving?"

"It's a girl, Doctor," Merrilee said quietly. "And it was sometime yesterday, I think. The first I really noticed that she was still was last night."

"No movement this morning?"

Merrilee shook her head. "I thought she was just sleeping. I didn't know anything was wrong."

"Of course you didn't." He touched her head lightly, smiling sadly.

"But what happened?" Nora said. How could everyone speak so calmly, so clinically?

"I'm not sure, Mrs. Rey. The ultrasound doesn't reveal any abnormality with the baby or the placenta. It's possible we may never know." He paused. "My main concern right now is that the baby be delivered. Whatever the cause of death, we don't want to put Merrilee in jeopardy, too."

"Delivered? But . . . but . . ."

"Merrilee, we can sedate you and do a C-section . . . do you know what that is?"

"Where you cut me open and take the baby out while I'm sleeping?"

He nodded. "Or we could give you drugs to induce labor. You'd be awake for that."

Nora turned her head away, shutting her eyes. What kind of choices was he offering Merrilee?

"I want to be awake," Merrilee said, her voice calm. "I want to see my baby being born." She turned toward Nora and Steven. "And I'd like you two with me . . . if you want to be."

"Of course we do, Merrilee," Steven said. He bent and kissed the girl's cheek.

Nora opened her eyes and looked at Merrilee. The girl's eyes pleaded with her own, and Nora felt as if her heart would break in two. *Oh, Merrilee!*

"I'm so sorry, Nora," she whispered, her eyes wet. "I'm so . . ." Sobbing, she laid her hands on her belly. "Oh, Baby Girl!"

Nora pressed a hand over Merrilee's, and Steven touched her shoulder. Nora bit back her own tears in deference to Merrilee's. "We'll be there," she said. "Whatever you want . . . we'll be there for you."

Suddenly everyone was all action. Mrs. Pennywood was located, and acting as Merrilee's guardian, she signed the necessary papers. An orderly and a nurse came down from an upper floor of the hospital to take Merrilee away in a wheelchair. A stout, fiftyish nurse promised that Nora and Steven could join her later.

"I want Nora to go with me," Merrilee said, clamping her hand around the wheelchair's brake lever.

"But, dear, she's not family. She's not even a legal guardian."

"I want her to go with me," Merrilee insisted in a low voice.

"Please?" Nora said. "I'm the adoptive mother of the baby. But more than that, I'm Merrilee's friend."

The nurse wavered. "All right. But only you. Your husband will have to wait until it's time for her to deliver. I'll take Merrilee up to the sixth floor. You can join us there." She signaled to the orderly, who hustled Merrilee into the elevator without giving her a chance to speak.

Steven kissed Nora on the cheek and drew her into his embrace. "Can I bring you anything? Something to read?"

She shut her eyes, wishing she could shut out the past hour as well. "Nothing, Steven." Her eyes watered. "I can't believe this is happening to her. She doesn't deserve this."

Steven held her closer. "Father," he whispered, "we don't understand why this is happening. We're grieving for the baby, but we're also grieving for Merrilee. She's just a girl, too young to go through this at all, much less with no parents to be with her. Help us to fill those shoes, and give us the strength and wisdom to walk through the valley of the shadow of death alongside her."

Steven gently released Nora. "I'll make a few phone calls; then I'll hang around the sixth-floor waiting room. They'll get me when it's time for Merrilee to go to the delivery room."

"It could take hours, Steven. Just because . . .

just because the baby's dead, it doesn't mean that this will go any faster."

"I'll call the office to have Mary reschedule all my appointments for the next few days. This is where I need to be."

"I love you." Her eyes filled with tears. "I love you so much."

"I love you too, Blondie," he whispered. "Give Merrilee my love. I'll be praying for you both."

Nora turned away, then back again. The walk to the elevator seemed impossibly long. "How am I going to help her?"

Steven held her close again. "You're just going to have to walk into the fiery furnace and trust that God is with you, Nora. That's all you can do. Now go to her. She needs you, and you need her. You're going to help each other."

The nurse, who said her name was Ingrid, had Merrilee hooked up to an IV in record time, even before she could panic at the sight of the needle. Merrilee was grateful to see Nora arrive.

"We were just getting started," Ingrid said

after introducing herself to Nora. "If either of you have any questions—any concerns at all—don't hesitate to speak up. I just started my shift, so I'll be on duty for twelve hours. I'll be your nurse exclusively, Merrilee, and I'll be with you from here until delivery, then afterward, okay?"

Merrilee nodded, pressing her lips together to keep from crying. If she started bawling, it would only make Nora feel bad.

Nora slipped her hand into hers, and Merrilee relaxed.

"I'm going to give you the drug—it's called Pitocin—that will bring on your labor. I'll be checking on you occasionally to see how the labor's progressing."

She paused, her expression sorrowful. "Honey, this is a bum deal, and I know you're hurting emotionally. I'm proud of you for wanting to see your baby born—I don't think you'll regret it later. I've never had a patient tell me she did."

"You've been through this before? With other women?" Merrilee said.

Ingrid nodded, fussing with the IV line. "Did you take a Lamaze class?"

Merrilee's eyes teared up. Thankfully, Nora answered for her. "We didn't get a chance."

"When we get to the hard part of labor, I'll be showing you how to breathe to help with the pain. And to calm yourself. Mrs. Rey, you can do them with Merrilee." Ingrid stepped away from the IV stand. "There. The Pitocin's started. I'll monitor the level to make sure your contractions aren't so far apart that nothing happens, or so close together that you can't catch your breath. If the pain does get too bad, we can give you a pill to relax you, or even a shot that will numb you from the waist down."

"I don't like shots," Merrilee mumbled.

Ingrid smiled in sympathy. "Just keep it in mind in case you want some relief. But don't wait too long because if you get the urge to push, it's too late then. Let me go check on a few things, ladies; then I'll be back."

When she'd gone, Nora pulled up a chair beside the bed. Merrilee stared at the IV, unable to look at her.

Drip, drip, drip.

Merrilee shut her eyes.

"Merrilee, I'm so sorry," Nora whispered. "This is such a shock, I don't know what else to say. What can I do for you?"

"Nothing."

Drip, drip.

They sat together, silent, for several hours. Merrilee kept her eyes squeezed shut.

The rippling began in her belly, pains so light at first that she scarcely noticed them.

At last Nora cleared her throat. "Can I call someone for you? Your friend Sylvie, maybe?"

"There's no one to call." Merrilee kept her eyes shut, and she imagined she could hear the liquid pouring into her veins, forcing her body to expel the baby.

She needed Mama to hold her and sing, to see her through this. But Mama was gone.

How they'd laugh back in Palmwood when she returned with an empty belly and the knowledge that her Baby Girl was dead.

"Nora?"

"Yes? I'm here."

"I didn't ever tell you about Mama's death."

"No, you didn't."

"Or about Wayne."

"No, you didn't tell me much about him, either."

"Mama was disappointed when she found out I was pregnant. She'd always told me to stay away from boys, get myself a good education, and become somebody. But when she knew about the baby, she told me to forget all that. That I was going to have to work, same as her, to support the baby."

"What about Wayne?" Nora said softly. "He could have at least contributed financially. It was his responsibility, as the father."

Merrilee felt a tear trickle from her eyes. The pains were increasing. "I didn't want anything to do with him. His daddy had been hanging out with Mama for a while, and one day when ol' Lucas came to visit, he brought his son, Wayne. Lucas wanted to be alone with Mama, so he gave Wayne some money and told him to treat me right. Just like that, he said,

'Treat her right, boy,' and laughed. Like they had some kind of joke between them."

"Then what happened?" Nora asked gently.

"It was the tail end of summer, still hot, so I put my bathing suit on under my clothes, and we headed for a stock pond off a country road. On the way there, Wayne stopped and bought some beer. I'd never had it before, but he said, go on, don't be a baby, and didn't my mama drink it?

"Anyway, I was feeling kind of good about having a fella notice me, even if his daddy did pay for him to do so. I popped a top and took a sip. He laughed and said, no, Merrilee, ya got to swallow it down real quick. By the time we got to the pond, I'd drunk two."

She heard Nora shift in the chair beside the bed. "Merrilee, you don't have to talk about this if you don't want to."

Merrilee bit back a groan.

Nora rose. "Are you having a contraction?"

She nodded, unable to speak for a moment. The pain was dull but fast, as if someone were closing a fist around her insides. When it subsided, she felt her breathing slow to normal and found the nurse beside her.

"The Pitocin's working," Ingrid said. "Let's have a look and see how far you've dilated."

She pulled back the sheet and examined Merrilee, who stared up at the acoustic tiles in the ceiling. Nora sat beside her, lending silent support.

"You're to four centimeters, almost to five," Ingrid said, lowering the sheet. "The contractions will start coming harder now. When they do, try breathing like this. Mrs. Rey, you watch too. It'll be easy for Merrilee to lose her focus, and you may need to get right down in her face and remind her."

They watched while Ingrid demonstrated; then they each practiced panting and hee-hee-hee-hoo-ing in rhythm. Ingrid smiled, then left—"Just for a bit because I think things are going to speed up soon."

When they were alone again, Merrilee leaned back and tried to collect her thoughts. She wanted to be ready when the pain came again. She also wanted to finish telling Nora the whole story. "You can probably figure out what happened."

"After that boy got you drunk?" Nora said.

Merrilee nodded. "At first it was fun. We were just goofing around, I thought, being silly. Then when I realized Wayne didn't have any intention of stopping, I got scared. He was acting mean, calling me a tease, saying I didn't have to act so innocent-like. Everybody knew what my mama was like and that I wasn't any different."

"But you were, Merrilee," Nora said softly. "And you still are."

The pain began again, low in Merrilee's insides. "It didn't matter. Even after he realized he'd been wrong, he looked real sorry but said no one would believe I'd told him no. If I wouldn't say anything, he wouldn't either.

"By the time he dropped me home, I was so sick, I went straight to bed. When I woke up the next morning, Lucas was still there. He winked and asked me if I'd had a good time with his son, and I knew then that he thought the same as Wayne had. That everybody did."

The pain rose. She sat up and let out a moan, the contraction cresting.

Nora got to her feet. "Breathe, Merrilee. Breathe."

Merrilee did, and when she'd made it through and lay back down, she was surprised to find she was crying. Nora stroked the wet hair back from her face. "What about your mother, Merrilee? Surely she believed you."

She shook her head. "Mama was hungover all day and didn't get up until suppertime. Then she had to get ready for her shift, and I tried to tell her, but she waved me off with one of her sick headaches. I waited up to talk when she came home, knowing she'd have drunk a bunch of coffee and be feeling better. But the first thing she said was, 'Well, Merrilee, I saw Wayne, and he said you two didn't hit it off yesterday. It's probably just as well, what with me seeing his daddy and all.'"

"But you told her the truth?"

Merrilee shook her head. "I figured it was over, and there was no point in being a crybaby about it."

"But you got pregnant. Surely then you told your mother."

"Not right away. Mama had a big falling-out with Lucas Procter. He'd taken up with some woman he'd met in a bar, and Mama regularly threatened to go shoot her, him, or both of them. Wayne had left town by then, and if Mama knew what he'd done to me, she might have gotten liquored up and shot his daddy instead."

Merrilee felt the next wave coming, and she braced herself. "Besides, she right away assumed I'd been agreeable with Wayne. And there she'd been trying to teach me to stay away from boys, study hard, and all that."

"Oh, Merrilee. She would have understood."

"No, ma'am. Mama was getting sadder and sadder every day. The men weren't coming around anymore, and she started drinking heavier. My being pregnant changed her whole attitude toward me. She stopped loving me, it seemed like, stopped singing songs to me at night like she used to, even when I was too old for such things. She started yelling at me, something she never used to do.

"Finally, one night, she yelled at me about something I'd done wrong, and she called me a tramp. I couldn't take it anymore, and I told her if I was a tramp, then she was the one who taught me, and did she even care that while she was boozing it up with Lucas Procter, his son was forcing himself on me?

"She got real quiet; then she started crying. I felt bad for having talked to her that way—she was out-of-her-head drunk and didn't know what she'd been saying. I tried to tell her I was sorry. She just held me close, pulled me into her lap, even, and rocked me for a long time. 'My little girl,' she said over and over.

"When she finally stopped crying, I thought everything would be okay then. She gave me some money and asked me to go up to the trailer park office and buy her some cigarettes. That she'd cook us some supper when I returned."

Merrilee's voice broke against the knifing pain. "I heard the shot when I was coming back. We all went running, but it was too late."

A sob tore from her throat, lifted to the tiled

ceiling, and fell into pieces around her. The pain took her away on sharp wings.

Nora stroked her hair, her wet cheeks, her hands, bending low to whisper. "I'm sorry, Merrilee. I'm so sorry. It's all right. I'm here."

Merrilee groped for Nora's arm. She wanted to ask her not to leave, that she couldn't bear it again.

"I'm here, Merrilee," she heard Nora's voice say, as if from a distance. Then her face was right next to hers. "Breathe, sweetie. Like this— remember? Hee-hee-hee . . ."

The pain rocketed inside her, and she tried to comply.

"You're a brave, strong girl, Merrilee," Nora said. "You're doing fine. You always have. You've done right by this baby. Jesus knows you have."

An image of the crucifixion flashed through Merrilee's mind, a terrible scene with darkness and lightning like something out of a horror movie. Then Mama's words returned, swift and sharp: *The pity of it is that you're making me shoulder this cross too.*

She'd shouldered it just long enough to accompany Merrilee to Calvary; then she'd left her only child alone.

My God, my God, why have you forsaken me?

"Mama!" she cried out, and the pain subsided, then returned double force.

"Her labor moved so quickly, they didn't have time to give her anything for the pain," Nora said hurriedly to Steven as they donned paper surgical clothes. "Even the nurse was surprised. She's prepping Merrilee now, and we're supposed to meet them in the delivery room."

"Is Merrilee all right—emotionally, I mean?"

Nora shook her head, and a tear splashed onto the paper mask.

"How about you, Nora?"

The door swung open. "Dr. and Mrs. Rey? You'd better hurry. The baby's crowning."

They followed the unfamiliar nurse to the delivery room. The entire room looked green, from the tiles on the walls and floor to the scrubs on Dr. Welch at the foot of the table and the nurses encouraging Merrilee. A plastic bassinet sat nearby. Farther away stood an unplugged warming table.

"Thank goodness you're here." Ingrid ushered them to Merrilee's side, where the girl reclined against a backrest. "She's been asking for you."

"I thought you wouldn't make it," Merrilee said, looking better now that she could fight the pain by pushing when the doctor commanded. She strained forward, her face contorting with the effort. "She's . . . almost . . . here."

"That's it, Merrilee," Dr. Welch said. "Push! Here're the shoulders. . . . Once more!"

Nora put her arms under Merrilee. "Come on, sweetie, push," she said. "You can do it."

"And here she is," Dr. Welch said, handing off Merrilee's baby to a waiting nurse with a towel while he finished up.

The room grew quiet. Too quiet. Nora was conscious of the absence of the usual bustle and cries associated with a baby's birth, and she blinked back tears.

Merrilee leaned back against the backrest to

catch her breath, and Nora wiped her brow. "Can you see her?" Merrilee whispered. "Is she pretty?"

"They'll bring her to you, Merrilee," Ingrid said, her voice somber. "Let them take a few measurements and clean her up a bit. Then you can hold her."

As Ingrid spoke, the nurse with the baby brought her to Merrilee and solemnly handed her over. Nora stood alongside and watched as Merrilee drew back the blanket to greet her perfectly formed, perfectly still baby girl.

Merrilee wept silently and held her close, while Nora turned into Steven's arms and released her own quiet tears.

❋ ❋ ❋

They brought the baby again to Merrilee's room, and she and Nora bathed her side by side, then dressed her in the white christening gown. They shared sad smiles when it dwarfed her small body.

"You haven't held her yet," Merrilee said, cradling the baby, touching her cheek with awe.

"It doesn't seem right somehow," Nora said, a lump in her throat. "I don't want to intrude."

Merrilee turned. "She's your baby, too." She handed her to Nora.

In her arms, the baby felt light, hardly more than a small pillow. Nora stared at the tiny, sweet face, and she swallowed hard. "You gave this baby everything, Merrilee. You gave her a chance she wouldn't have had with a girl who'd chosen abortion."

"I guess it didn't matter much, though, did it?" Merrilee said bitterly. "Maybe it would have been better for all of us if that's what I'd chosen way back there."

"You chose a harder road."

"One that cost Mama her life."

"That was your mother's choice, Merrilee. Not yours," Nora said quietly. "What matters is that even though this baby's conception and life inside your womb caused great pain, you loved her without reservation."

Nora's eyes welled with tears, and she handed the baby back. "And grace is never cheap. Or easy. Ask God."

* * *

Merrilee did. During the next day that they kept
her in the hospital, while the hospital photo-
grapher took a photo and snipped a lock of her
daughter's hair as a keepsake, while the doctor
sadly said they couldn't determine the cause of
death, while she held her baby one last time and
wept when she handed her over to be cremated,
she asked God.

What had she done wrong? Hadn't she
turned the other cheek when others cast stones?
Hadn't she always chosen the baby ahead of
herself? Hadn't she always taken care of Mama
. . . ?

*Oh, Mama. Now I have two gaping places in my heart that
can never be filled.*

Steven and Nora brought her flowers, a small
vase with pale, full roses. She wanted to thank
them, but she could barely speak, could barely
endure their presence. They were grieving, too,
she knew, but the sorrow on their faces only
intensified the guilt in her heart. She'd let them
down, too.

When the doctor said she was well enough to

go home, Merrilee filled a paper bag with her meager belongings. Mrs. Pennywood would pick her up, then take her back to Adoption Lifeline.

"You can stay for a few days, if you need to think about things," she'd said.

But Merrilee knew she couldn't spend one night in a home filled with pregnant girls such as she'd been. Her stomach felt empty and gnawing.

"Merrilee?" Nora knocked on the half-open door, then entered. Steven followed closely behind, carrying a large bag. "You're packing?" Nora said.

"They're booting me out," Merrilee said, trying to smile. "Mrs. Pennywood should be here soon." She tossed a comb, the final item, into the bag. "I'm catching a bus this afternoon for home."

"Palmwood?" Steven said.

She nodded, then sat on the edge of the bed, unable to meet their gazes. Nora sat beside her and touched her shoulder. "We have another suggestion, one we hope you'll like." She glanced at Steven, smiling. "We want you to come live with us."

Merrilee raised her eyes. "What do you mean, live with you?"

"We're interested in becoming your legal guardians, Merrilee," Steven said. "Perhaps, in time—if you're willing—to even adopt you."

Merrilee's heart lifted, then fell. "That's a crazy idea."

"Is it?" Nora said. "We've gotten to know each other in a short period of time. Not to mention that we've shared the loss of your child."

"You should be trying to adopt another baby," Merrilee mumbled.

"We can't," Nora said simply.

"That's right. You're getting too old."

"We want you, Merrilee," Steven said quietly.

Merrilee's eyes filled with tears. Steven and Nora had worked their way into her heart and even now wouldn't leave. "I don't want to be the booby prize you win because you didn't get your first choice."

"Is that what you think?" Nora smiled sadly. "Merrilee, I was wondering how I was going to

let you go after the baby was born! And now
. . ." She shook her head. "Now we have even
more in common, more that's entwined our
lives. For years I thought God intended me to
receive—a baby. And you've thought he was
asking you to give up yours. But he's calling
me to give to you, Merrilee, and for you to
receive. From me. It's his blessing for each of
us—to be together."

"I shouldn't have told you about Wayne—and
Mama," Merrilee said.

"Why? Because you think I pity you now?"

"Well . . ."

"I'm sorry those things happened to you, but
I admire you more than I pity you. Pity is for
people who can't help themselves. You're the
strongest person I know, Merrilee. I'd like you
as my daughter because I could learn from you.
As well as, hopefully, teach you in return."

"It wouldn't work, Nora," Merrilee said. "I'm
sorry. Our connection was the baby, and now
she's gone."

"Did you name her, Merrilee?" Steven said.

"Yeah. When they brought around the papers

for me to sign, I listed her name as Grace. I thought about what y'all said about my loving her and sacrificing for her. I hope, at least, she knew she had all that going for her."

"I'm sure she did." Steven smiled.

"Well." Merrilee rose and picked up the bag. She had to get out of here—fast. Her hand rested briefly on the smaller stomach under her maternity blouse. "Mrs. Pennywood will be here soon. I think the nurse said I have to leave in a wheelchair, even though I feel perfectly capable of walking."

"There's nothing we can say to change your mind?" Steven said.

"Nothing to convince you that we only want to share a bit of the same grace with you that you shared with your daughter?" Nora added.

Merrilee shook her head, blinking back tears.

Nora hugged her, trying hard to smile. "I love you, Merrilee," she whispered. "You will always be the child of my heart. Know that I'm praying for you daily."

Merrilee nodded silently. Nora stepped away, wiping her eyes.

Steven withdrew two packages—one small, one large. "We wanted you to have these," he said. "The large one has been for you—Nora's planned to give it to you for a while but hasn't had a chance. The other was for the baby. We thought you should have it."

He kissed her on the cheek, and she saw her own sorrow reflected in his eyes. "Good-bye, Merrilee. If you ever need anything, you know where we are."

Steven took his wife's arm, and they left the room.

Merrilee sat on the bed, her vision blurred. She opened the first package to find a Nancy Drew mystery, the next one she needed in the series.

With trembling fingers, she opened the next package to find a white shiny box.

Inside was a small, sterling silver–filigreed jewelry box in the shape of a heart. When she lifted the lid, a lullaby wafted out.

Jesus loves me, this I know . . .

Merrilee shut the lid and gripped the box tightly.

chapter
SIX

$\mathscr{N}$ora listlessly spooned dog food into Lucky's dish. He wagged his tail, nearly upsetting his water dish. "We haven't been around much lately, have we, boy?" she said, scratching him behind his ears. "We'll get back into the swing of things, I guess."

She rinsed the can before tossing it in the recycling bin, then stared at the papasan chair. She should have given it to Merrilee.

Steven put his arm around her. "I suppose you're going to say I told you so," Nora said bitterly. "My heart's been broken twice in the past few days."

He kissed her temple, saying nothing.

Nora turned into his arms and rested her cheek against his chest. No matter how great her grief, she would never forget that Merrilee's was greater.

Jesus, comfort Merrilee now. Remind her that you love her.

Lucky looked up from his food and barked. A car door slammed, and the dog raced for the front door. Whining, he scratched the paint with his claws.

Steven glanced out the front window, then smiled at Nora. He nodded, as if in answer to her unspoken question.

Nora moved to the door, her pulse racing. In her haste to get outside, she neglected to hold Lucky back. The dog shot out the door and jumped on Merrilee, who was trying to pay the cabbie. Sizing up the German shepherd, the cab driver jumped into his car, tossed Merrilee's suitcase and the paper bag out the window, and sped away.

Merrilee turned and faced Nora and Steven. When they didn't speak, she looked down at the ground.

Nora moved forward and embraced her, her eyes filling with tears. After a long moment, Merrilee pulled back. "Is the invitation still good?" she whispered.

Nora cupped Merrilee's chin and gently raised her face. The scar on the bridge of her nose glistened, and Nora brushed back her hair. She was beautiful, so beautiful—the child of her dreams all these years. "Of course," she said, then couldn't speak for the emotion tightening her throat.

Merrilee glanced at Steven. "If it's okay . . . ?" she said hesitantly.

He nodded, then wrapped his arms around them both, his throat working up and down.

Lucky barked, started to jump into the group, then instead sat back on his haunches, whining. He followed the group as they gathered Merrilee's bags and together headed inside the house.

* * *

Dear Baby Girl,
This is the last time I'm going to write. So much has happened, but then you know all

that. Sometimes I think maybe you're watching from heaven, but other times I believe you're having too much fun with Jesus and everybody else to concern yourself with what's going on here.

But I do know that one day we'll meet face-to-face. You'll be much bigger, of course, but somehow I'll know you and you'll know me. I hope you're the one who takes my hand and introduces me to Jesus. I can't wait to meet both of you.

Meanwhile, Nora's calling, and I have to go. She's built a fire in the fireplace, and we're going to have a little ceremony of burning this journal. Today, you see, would have been your first birthday. She and I have talked and worked through a lot of things together. Steven too. We're all trying to look forward, not back, though of course I'll never forget you.

I haven't written in this journal since before you left this earth, but I wanted to give it back to you. Will you catch the ashes as they rise in the air? I hope they are a pleasing aroma to God, as well, because he is the only one who could have shown me such Grace.

I love you always and hope you rest in Jesus' arms so that he can sing all the lullabies you want. I know he does for me.

Your mother,
Merrilee Hunter Rey

About the Author

Jane Orcutt is a native Texan who currently resides in the Dallas—Fort Worth metroplex. She homeschools her two sons and is an ardent Texas Rangers baseball fan who still has trouble understanding the infield-fly rule and how to calculate the Magic Number.